PRAISE FOR *The Fat Years*

'Chan's story is not only absorbing in its own right,
it also shines reflected light on the foibles of the West'
New York Times

'A fascinating tale of China just over the horizon'
New Yorker

'A not-so-veiled satire of the Chinese government's tendency to
make dates such as the Tiananmen massacre virtually disappear'
Financial Times

'Bracing, smart and entertaining'
Independent

'An inventive and highly topical novel . . . among the
first to explore a scenario that much of the
world is speculating about today'
Wall Street Journal

'Chan Koonchung's humorous tale reveals the distorted reality
of China, where despite the supersonic development of its
economy, political life remains steadfastly unchanging'
Ma Jian

'Anyone who ~~wants to understand~~ modern
~~...~~ is novel'

www.transworldbooks.co.uk

D1054019

Also by Chan Koonchung

THE FAT YEARS

and published by Black Swan

The Unbearable Dreamworld of Champa the Driver

CHAN KOONCHUNG

Translated from the Chinese by Nicky Harman

BLACK SWAN

TRANSWORLD PUBLISHERS
61–63 Uxbridge Road, London W5 5SA
www.transworldbooks.co.uk

Transworld is part of the Penguin Random House group of companies
whose addresses can be found at global.penguinrandomhouse.com

Penguin
Random House
UK

First published in Great Britain in 2014 by Doubleday
an imprint of Transworld Publishers
Black Swan edition published 2015

A CIP catalogue record for this book
is available from the British Library.

ISBN
9780552779500

Typeset in Berling by Kestrel Data, Exeter, Devon.
Printed and bound by CPI Group (UK) Ltd, Croydon, CR0 4YY.

Penguin Random House is committed to a sustainable future
for our business, our readers and our planet. This book is made
from Forest Stewardship Council® certified paper.

1 3 5 7 9 10 8 6 4 2

The Unbearable Dreamworld of
Champa the Driver

PART ONE

Flesh

Chapter One

1

LIFE'S A bitch. That was one of Plum's little sayings.

Plum was always trotting out some colourful expression or other. At first, my Chinese wasn't so good and I didn't pay much attention. But then I gradually figured them out. In fact, I learned them off by heart because I thought they were really interesting.

Expressions like, 'Life's a bitch', 'It's serendipity', 'You're a sex fiend!', and 'It's bear-faced wickedness!' . . .

If Plum said: 'How the hell did I meet a sex fiend like you?', I'd say: 'It was serendipity.' Then she'd look at me, all bright-eyed, and nod: 'Yeah, it's serendipity . . .' We were always going on like that. Plum was full of fun. I liked it when she was enjoying herself, because she was super-nice to me then.

Sometimes, if she was browsing the web or tweeting, and she read some bad news, she'd look sad and sigh: 'Life's a bitch . . . It's bear-faced wickedness.' Then she'd get fired up: 'I hope those bastards' mouths go rotten and their teeth fall out!'

I loved her sense of justice and compassion. She had strong emotions and she'd always fly to the defence of the underdog. But she was good to anyone, rich or poor, Chinese or Tibetan.

Then there was another expression, 'Blood's sicker than water.' Once, Mr Ouyang took some clients from Taiwan out to a meal, and Plum and I went too. When everyone had had plenty to drink, Mr Ouyang proclaimed: 'We're all blood brothers, all one big family!' And they stood up and flung their arms around each other, and Plum went: 'Yup, blood's sicker than water!' Then they all started shouting: 'Blood's sicker than water! Blood's sicker than water!' I was over on the sofa, making a pot of tea for them, and I didn't understand what they were shouting about. But the expression did make me laugh. It reminded me of the lamas saying you can achieve enlightenment if you conserve the tantric juices. A few days later, Plum and I went to buy steaks from the Muslim butchers in Tromsikhang Market. Great lumps of freshly slaughtered beef were laid out on the stalls, and bloody water dripped on to the ground. And then it just popped out of my mouth: 'Blood's sicker than water!' I was just teasing Plum, it was a bit of fun, but she pulled a disgusted face at me. But I reckon I'd got it right . . . I mean, whether you say 'blood's sicker than water', or 'conserve the tantric juices', it's all to do with flesh. When you've got flesh, you've got water, and water and flesh make blood, sick blood too, and that's what all living beings, including us humans, are made of. To a tiger, humans are just meat, and to a mozzy, we're just blood. That business about 'conserving tantric juices' is a bit obscure, though. Now the way the Chinese say it, 'blood's sicker than water,' that's it, in a nutshell. It's really fucking cool. What it means is, all us humans are basically the same. We're all fine and there's no difference between us. Each one of us is just a lump of meat, sick blood and water. We're all brothers, so give me a hug!

(It was only much later, when my Chinese got better, that I realized I'd got Plum's sayings just a little bit wrong.)

2

Plum said she was getting chubby, but I liked her chubby. Her body was as smooth as satin and you couldn't feel any bones. She said she was from south China so she had a small frame. I couldn't tell a southern Chinese from a northern one, but I knew she was different from most Chinese women. She told me that she'd really had satiny smooth skin when she was young, but I couldn't imagine skin smoother than what she had now. When I was on top of her, kneading her all over, with my cock pushing in and out of her cunt, I couldn't feel a single bone. And when she took my cock in her mouth, though she didn't do that often, it felt like she had no teeth either. She was, like, pure flesh.

We got on so well together.

Her body was a mass of nerve endings. If I gave her ear a lick, or nipped her shoulder, she'd go, 'No, no, I can't bear it! It's like being struck by lightning!'

Mostly, I waited for her before I came off, but I never had to wait long. It was easy for her, she'd climax just like that.

When she was getting near, she'd shriek and shriek, and then a great growl came from deep in her throat. To tell you the truth, when we first got together, that scared me a bit, her shrieking and growling, but I soon got used to it. She felt good about herself and I liked that. She would really let rip. Most of the women I'd slept with before couldn't let themselves go like that. I don't reckon she was born that way, it was definitely something she'd learned from being with lots of men. She could satisfy herself and satisfy the men who fucked her. And when Plum was enjoying herself, I enjoyed myself. When she came, I felt I was the dog's bollocks.

If she had an especially good time, she used to call me a 'sex fiend'.

On top, underneath, from behind and face-to-face. If she was on top, she'd say afterwards: 'Your turn to do the work next time.'

I 'worked' almost every day when Plum was around.

My tantric juices were getting put to good use.

'How did you happen to me?' she asked me once. I said it was 'serendipity'. 'Yes,' she said. 'It was serendipity, Champie Baby.'

Usually it was her who started it. Sometimes she'd give me a little scratch with her finger; other times, she'd hiss at me like a snake. When she was in a good mood, the usual signal was a couple of winks followed by a naughty little look. I knew that meant she wanted it and it made me hard immediately.

And we'd go straight to bed.

She said she had a 'thing' about beds. Our bed and the mattress were both imported, and very sturdy, so you could bounce as much as you liked.

Sometimes I'd be in the middle of having a pee, and she'd put her arms around me from behind and hold me. Or, if I was in the shower, she'd undress and get in too, and soap me all over and play with me, and we'd end up having sex in the bathroom. 'Spur of the moment' was what she called that. Once I said 'spurt of the moment' and she corrected me: '"Spur" not "spurt"!' But from then on, we called it a 'spurt of the moment' anyway.

And sometimes we'd do a 'spurt of the moment' outdoors, in a park.

But mostly that super-cool bed at home was our battlefield. We spent a lot of time every day in bed, each with our own iPad. Plum liked to watch TV, I surfed car websites or played computer games; she watched the news, I surfed car websites or played computer games; she tweeted, I surfed car websites or played computer games; she muttered 'life's a bitch' or 'bear-faced wickedness', I would say 'Yay! Gimme five!' Of course, we spent most of the time grappling and 'working'. We both liked sleeping, too. Sometimes, when she was tired, she'd say 'I'm really bushed' but I never worked out what she meant by that.

Three years went by.

We could have gone on like that.

I wish we had.

After Plum, I never had such a good time with any woman.

But things changed. Three years passed, and it began to be her who started things. It was less and less often that I made the first move.

3

Our relationship had started when she had to go to the airport one day and called my taxi. Four years ago, there was no expressway to Gonggar Airport. She spent ages getting ready and, when we set off, there was an accident and we got snarled up in traffic. I tried every shortcut I knew but I couldn't make up the time. When we got to the airport, I had a feeling she'd missed the flight so I waited for her outside. Sure enough, she soon came out again, dragging her suitcase and looking pissed off. She was delighted when she saw I'd waited for her, and I drove her back home. After that, every time she went on a trip, she got me to drive her to and from the airport. Then she offered me a job as her driver. I drove her 4x4, and did errands for her, and she paid me a monthly wage.

I worked out that I could earn more with her than driving for a tour agency. She seemed decent and I liked driving. Besides, there wasn't much pressure. When she was away from Lhasa, she carried on paying me but I had practically nothing to do. She said: 'Look after the car for me when I'm not here, and water the plants at home every other day.' She didn't ask the cleaning woman to water her plants, she asked me.

From the very first day she took me on as her driver, I had sexual fantasies about her, though I'd never had those kinds of fantasies before. I always thought I was attracted to slim girls and didn't like chubby ones. I'd never had a chubby girlfriend, just skinny ones. Plum was slightly built but she was well covered. Not fat, just well covered. Still, as our foreign friends used to say, she wasn't 'my type'.

How the hell did it happen? She was much older than me and I wasn't into older women. I was once the driver for a sexologist from Hong Kong, and he told me all about sexual fetishes, things I'd never imagined in my life. I thought I was pretty normal, I liked girls, and for completely natural reasons, to get them into bed, however you would prefer to express that. Foreigners would say 'Fuck you!' Beijingers and Hong Kongers would say it differently, but it all meant the same thing.

I could write the Chinese characters for 'fuck'. Lhasa was a centre of international tourism.

In summer, Plum used to wear cotton or linen outfits with silk or cotton scarves draped round her shoulders. She always had something on that was brightly coloured – red, purple or yellow especially. She had loads of hats, which she wore to keep the sun off, different hats to go with different outfits. She wore tight pedal-pusher slacks, and T-shirts. She said she bought all her clothes in Nepal, Burma, Hong Kong and Beijing. She never wore Tibetan clothes, she didn't like the colours, but she had a lot of Tibetan jewellery. She had necklaces and bracelets of *dzi* beads and agate, turquoise and amber, diamond rings, box-shaped silver lockets made for holding religious relics, bronze Vajra knots and amulets, gold Omega and Cartier watches, all kinds of things. She had full ear lobes, but her ears weren't pierced, and I could pull her earrings off with my lips. She had good skin and her face glowed. She painted her fingernails and toenails but wore no make-up except lipstick and sun-cream. Her hair was long and slightly wavy. She looked classy, and friendly at the same time, and just . . . womanly. The first day I went to work, she came down the narrow stairs, wearing a white T-shirt, and I could see her tits wobbling underneath . . .

Suddenly I felt horny.

From that moment on, I had sex on the brain. I particularly noticed the way those heavyweight breasts of hers bounced up and down. I noticed, the way I hadn't before, that her arse (and her breasts, of course), and even her calves, her ear lobes, fingers, toes and nose, were all nicely rounded . . . everything that ought to be nice and round in a woman was nice and round, and everything that ought to stick out stuck out. She often had a slight smile on her face, and that made the left-hand corner of her rosy red lips turn upwards. In the bright Lhasa sunshine, I could see that there was a small mole on her lip. She must have been stunning when she was younger. She still was stunning, a real knock-out.

Of course, I knew my position and kept myself under control. I worked all day and wanked at night, and by the next day I'd calmed down again.

I don't know when she started to look at me that way. Maybe it was one day during the River Bathing Festival in September, the first year I worked for her. She had a client visiting from China that afternoon and they went out drinking. Then she went home to change, and, still tipsy, she was off out again to a banquet. We drove by the river. Venus was visible in the dark night sky.

'Look!' Plum exclaimed. 'There are people in the river, even though it's so cold.' I told her it was the Bathing Festival. 'Oh! So they're not wearing any clothes?'

'That's right,' I said. 'We like not wearing clothes. Do you want to stop and take a look?'

There was a moment's silence and Plum laughed: 'Idiot! Do you think all Chinese are Peeping Toms?'

'No! I never thought the Chinese were Peeping Toms!' I protested but then I added a bit lamely: 'I mean, I thought it was just human nature . . .'

'Champie, you're getting very naughty,' Plum said.

It must have been that evening that the prayer flags stirred in the wind and it all started between us.

Most evenings, when Plum had dinner and drank with friends, I found somewhere nearby to wait for her. But that evening, she invited me to have dinner with her and the client, and introduced me as her assistant.

From that day on, she started to call me Champie in front of everyone. The nickname made me feel uncomfortable but it was too late to object.

But maybe it was before the festival that her feelings changed. One day I parked the car in her company's courtyard to give it a wash. It was a 2009, dark green, series 200 Toyota A-Land Cruiser 4x4 SUV, five doors, six speed, 4.7 litre, V8 engine. I took the mat out and shook it. Then I left it out in the sun and opened the car up for an airing to get rid of the smell of cigarettes. People say that Tibetans don't mind body smells, but we Lhasa folk are not like that. I didn't like those smells and I knew Plum didn't either. Neither of us smoked and we didn't like the car smelling of fags but we couldn't stop the clients smoking in the car. I had a bit of time so I swept out the inside and brushed along the cracks between the seats. In the reflection from the car door, I could see Plum standing nearby, watching me. It was a while before she came over saying, as if she'd just seen me: 'You here already? We'll leave in ten minutes.'

Or it might have been even a bit earlier than that, otherwise why would she have taken me on as her driver? She spent six months in every year away from Lhasa, and up till then she'd always driven her own car.

However it was, for the first few months she didn't give me any signal. I was the one who kept having fantasies about her. Of course, when I was working, I remembered my place.

She liked her food, did Plum. She ate anything – Tibetan, Nepalese, halal, Sichuanese, Cantonese, steaks, Buddhist vegetarian, even fast-food fried chicken, and hotpot. She loved numbing-hot Sichuan pepper dishes, and started to invite me along to share them. 'Come for a Chongqing hotpot with me, Champie. I can't eat a whole hotpot on my own,' was how she put it. If she had no business dinners in the evening, then she'd get me to pick her up and we'd go for a meal. When she'd had a good dinner, she'd exclaim: 'I'm putting on weight!' as if putting on weight was a slow torture. Actually, eating out with Plum was making me put on weight too, and I was getting a chubby face and a paunch.

I didn't know what other people thought until a friend said people were calling me Plum's 'Tibetan mastiff puppy'. But I didn't care.

I could cook simple dishes myself. In Lhasa, the men cooked for the family when the women went out drinking. Married women often went out on the town together, dressed in their fancy costumes and coloured *pangden* aprons, and came back home tipsy. Folk from out-of-town couldn't believe their eyes, especially the ones from places like Kham and Amdo. My friend from Kham said that Lhasa men gave men a bad name because they were so lax.

I told Plum I could cook a stir-fry. She didn't look too impressed until I said it was a Sichuan stir-fry. Then she invited me back to her place to make dinner.

That evening, when I was cooking in the kitchen, Plum came up behind and put her arms around me. I took her hand and made her hold my cock. At least, that's how I fantasized the scene later on.

What actually happened was this: she came into the kitchen just as I was rinsing the rice and getting ready to pressure-cook it. 'Stop that,' she said. 'Mr Ouyang has invited a writer from Beijing out for a meal. Let's go.' And the next day, she was off to Kathmandu.

A week later she was back. On the way home from the airport, she said: 'Come over to my place for a steak tomorrow, OK?'

The next evening I bought some bread, and off I went to her house. The sitting room and dining room were all neat and tidy, and the table was laid with steak knives and forks, thousand island dressing, *wasabi* and so on. I went into the kitchen to wait for her.

Soon I heard Mr Ouyang drive up to the house, with Plum in the car. I found this a bit strange but Plum said: 'I went to Mr Ouyang's for some red wine. I was going to walk back, but he insisted on driving me.' She had two bottles of red wine in her hands.

'Why didn't you get me to drive you there and back?' I asked, but for some reason she didn't answer.

She opened the fridge and took out the prepared vegetables. Then she pointed to some raw steaks sitting on the counter. 'I've made a potato salad and the steaks are all ready. I'll fry them now. I don't know if the meat's any good, but we'll just have to make do. There are some Chinese leaves and carrots, I'll slice them and we can dip them in the dressing. You slice the bread and put it in the bread basket.'

It didn't sound very appetising to me, so I said: 'Let me slice some pickles and add some chilli and black beans and I'll stir-fry the leaves.' Plum looked at me, and the left corner of her lip curved upwards but she said nothing so I went on: 'Let me do the dinner. You just get on with whatever you've got to do.' 'Is that OK?' 'Sure! Shut the kitchen door behind you so the fumes don't get into the sitting room.'

There were plenty of fumes when I stir-fried chillies. It was choking. There was no way Plum would come up behind and grab me. You're hopeless, I told myself.

I fried two steaks and sliced the other two to stir-fry with the leaves. Then I cut up some big cloves of garlic and put them into the pan. I knew it would taste good.

She gave a small smile as I brought the food to the table. I sat down and we clinked glasses. 'This is good French wine,' she said. I had a gulp and didn't like it much, but I took another gulp anyway. I always liked any kind of alcohol.

I poured more wine for us and pointed to the food. 'Your cooker's not hot enough,' I said. 'You should get a Chinese-style kitchen. Fancy flats in Chengdu all have kitchens that you can close off from the rest of the house, just right for Chinese-style cooking. That's what you need for making really good food.'

'You haven't done anything the way I planned it,' said Plum.

I had a sudden feeling that something was different today. Plum raised her glass again. 'Bottoms up,' I said.

I gulped down half a glass of red wine. Plum smiled and emptied her glass too.

Maybe I'd drunk it too fast, but the wine suddenly made me feel elated. I dived into the food. Plum wasn't eating much but she was very complimentary about my cooking.

I was pleased and we clinked glasses again. We carried on with our food. 'Do you think the steaks are a bit tough?' she asked. 'They're not that great,' I said. 'Next time I'll buy them for you.' She hadn't touched the stir-fried carrot and beef. 'Try this,' I suggested. 'The beef slices are tender.' But she refused. 'I don't fancy garlic today.'

I opened the other bottle. Plum said: 'Go easy on the wine. I want to talk.'

I poured myself a full glass and held on to it as I listened to her. 'You know, Champie,' she began, 'lots of things in this world are serendipity. You can't force good things. They happen if both sides are willing partners. Do you know what I mean?'

I nodded. 'Now listen to what I've been thinking,' she went on. 'If you don't agree, then that's that. I don't want to force anything on you. I'm a tough woman, I can take it. You've got to be honest with me. I can give you all the time you need to think about it. The important thing is to make the right decision. "Act in haste, repent at leisure" as they say.'

I looked at the label on the wine bottle. It was only 14 per cent alcohol. How had I got so pissed?

'On my visit to Nepal, I went to a monastery and talked to the Rinpoche,' she went on. 'I asked him about us. I asked him, if we both want this – and I want to make sure you really want it – will there be any problem in us being together? The Rinpoche was quite clear about it. He said there would be no problem. He just told me to do the Four Preparatory Stages of Training.'

I heard every word Plum said but somehow I wasn't taking it in. Wanting, not wanting, problems, no problems, I thought I understood, but then again I didn't really. I emptied my glass, filled and raised it again.

'The Rinpoche was being kind,' Plum went on. 'The Four

Preparatory Stages of Training are for my own benefit, because the prostrations will help me lose weight.'

Then she cut up some steak and put it in my bowl. I let her serve me without protest. Plum's drunk as much as I have, how come she's sober and I'm pissed as a newt? I wondered. I wasn't going to let myself be defeated by wine of 14 per cent, I was quite sure of that. I crammed a big piece of steak into my mouth. Plum said nothing more, just glanced at me and gave a little smile.

Then she got up, her glass in her hand: 'Let's go and sit on the sofa.' I didn't follow her but just shifted my chair around, left one arm resting on the table and looked at Plum sitting on the other side of the room.

Facing me, Plum sipped her wine, then put it down, still looking at me, smiling, looking . . . I smiled back. Then Plum winked at me. I stared and smiled. Then she held out her arms to me.

I suddenly came to my senses, and threw myself on her, pulling her clothes off, kissing and rubbing her all over. First her face, her ears, her lips, then her shoulders, then all over her body, and Plum was moaning: 'Oh, oh, I've been struck by lightning! It's killing me!' And I'm thinking: 'Oh God, I'm so horny, it's killing me.' I was covering her in spittle, and the more I licked the more I had. And she was wet down there, soaking wet, I could see her clitoris, swollen like a little cherry, and I pushed my fingers inside her and wriggled them around. She writhed under me, and yelled like a madwoman, and then a great growl came from deep in her throat. I was suddenly wide awake – really, this time – as Plum came, in one great magnificent orgasm. Her face was flushed pink and she lay back helpless on the sofa, gazing at me in a puzzled way, like a little girl. The effects of the wine had completely worn off. I stood up, pulled my trousers down and looked at her. I pressed her backwards and shoved my cock hard into her. Plum was going, 'No, no, it hurts,' and trying to push me away but I ignored her, and soon she was wet again, and yelling like a mad woman, and she came again.

So that was how it started. It was that evening Plum first called me a sex fiend.

4

When we were together, we spent two or three days each week at home and made our own meals. I'm not a bad cook, I just don't like washing the vegetables, so sometimes she did that bit. But mostly I offered to wash them and told her to get on with her work. After all, I didn't have much to do.

And Plum had lots to do. She was a good businesswoman, everyone said so, good at making money and a good provider too. She had fingers in every pie. Besides her Beijing business interests, she'd spent ten years trading in Tibet in Buddhist statuettes and ritual objects, antiques and *dzi* beads, caterpillar fungus and saffron, and then she'd expanded into Hong Kong as well. She said she wanted to diversify into tourism, organizing tour groups in jeeps, and investing in high-quality boutique hotels. Then it was mining.

Mining was the real money-spinner, Plum said. Rumour had it that she and a partner had opened a mine in Shigatse. They'd then sold it on to a big corporation and made a packet.

The 'Stability Preservation' campaign brought lots of jobs to Lhasa, as new businesses opened to cater for increased numbers of Communist Party officials. Plum was always being asked to open luxury restaurants and clubs for them. But she said she didn't want to get involved with officialdom any more than was strictly necessary. She also said that the current lot of Chinese officials posted to Tibet were just layabouts who spent their time drinking, gambling and whoring while waiting to be promoted to a better job back home. They didn't do any work and were always on the take.

Recently Plum had been saying that she didn't want to have all her eggs in one basket. There was too much unrest and a heavy army presence in Tibet, and any new unrest would keep the tourists and business people away. She needed to invest elsewhere, so she set up a mining enterprise in Nepal (the idea was to pave the way for Chinese government investment) and there were projects in Burma too. That was while it was still closed to the outside world so she could have the field to herself . . . I'm not expressing myself very clearly, but that was the sort of stuff she was discussing anyway.

She saw I was at a loose end and asked me if I'd like to open a bar. My gut instinct made me say no. Lhasa was such a small place that everyone knew everyone. When I went out for a night on the town, I liked to go to someone else's place. There was no need to run my own. I didn't like the idea of poaching business from my friends either.

Plum was cool about that. 'It doesn't matter, Champie,' she said. 'If you don't want to, then don't.'

When she was in Lhasa, I went everywhere with her. I was her driver, cook, housekeeper, private assistant and toyboy. I loved driving her around. She liked temples, she'd been to lots, and every year she'd visit some elderly lamas she knew, to give them gifts of tonics and medicines. I liked going out drinking with her, and singing along to Faye Wong in *karaoke* bars. In the early days, we often used to go to a *nangma* club to hear the singing. Nowadays she spent a lot of time wining and dining business clients and officials. Sometimes she took me along too, and she'd introduce me as her assistant. I didn't say much, mostly I spent my time filling up their wine glasses, making tea and lighting clients' cigarettes and then driving them home when they'd had too much to drink. Everyone accepted me. I really admired Plum, she worked hard and played hard and Tibetans and Chinese all wanted to be her friends. She taught me a lot, especially how to behave properly. She always knew what people wanted and arranged it for them. She said that in business both sides had to be willing partners. She offered to give me the capital to set up a business on my own, but I said no, I just wanted to learn things from her.

I did want to go to Nepal and Burma with her but I had no passport. I applied but I couldn't get one, no reason given. If you were Tibetan they wouldn't discuss it, they just didn't want ordinary Tibetans going abroad. Plum said not to worry, she'd think of a way of getting me a passport.

A few times I said to Plum I'd like to go with her to Beijing to, you know, look around, get to know the place, see what I could do. Plum just let the subject drop. But that was my dream – if I could get to Beijing, the world was my oyster.

Every time she went to Beijing or Hong Kong to fix up a deal, or to Nepal or Burma on business, I felt at a loose end. I didn't like going out on my own so I spent all day at home, surfing the web, looking at cars and playing games, sometimes washing the car or taking it out for a spin, and watering the plants every other day, keeping the cosmos and geranium bushes looking bright and perky.

All the time I was at home, I was practising drinking red wine. She'd bought a cool box, apparently recommended by Mr Ouyang, which kept the red wine at a constant temperature of 14 degrees even in Lhasa.

Even if she was going to be away just a couple of days, she left money for me, five or ten thousand *yuan*, and told me to spend it on whatever I wanted. I never spent that much so when she came home, I gave it back to her. She wanted me to keep it but I told her I had no use for it. She'd say: 'What a good boy you are, Champie.'

She bought all my clothes for me in Beijing: T-shirts, jeans, trainers, watches, windcheaters. They were all the most fashionable foreign brands, but straight from the factory so they weren't expensive. And she told me not to buy fake labels in Lhasa any more. She said she'd seen a genuine Harley leather jacket she was going to get for me. She gave me a credit card. When she got herself a new Korean-made mobile phone, she gave me the iPhone she'd only had for a few months. She put a year's credit on it, and it had 3G so I could browse anywhere in China.

At the beginning of February, Plum took a trip to Beijing. Normally, she was only away a week or so and she planned to be back by the Tibetan New Year later in the month. But this New Year, foreigners were refused entry permits. The same happened in March, because this month was the anniversary of the Dalai Lama's departure from Tibet and so it was a 'politically sensitive' time, and the government thought there would be demonstrations. Even if Lhasa was completely peaceful, the ban wouldn't be lifted till April. This was when I found out that Plum had a Hong Kong ID. Originally, Hong Kong and Macao residents could come to Tibet just like other Chinese, but under the new policy Hong Kongers were being kept out, at least for now.

We talked on the phone every day. I'm fine, I said, and I've still got money left. Don't worry. 'Is that little guy missing me?' she asked. I couldn't very well say it wasn't, but if I said it was, then she might think I was up to no good. I told her the little guy was bushed. I must have said the right thing, because she laughed.

I wondered if I should drop in at the shop and see how things were going and pass on any messages, but Plum said not to bother, she talked to them on WeChat every day. Plum's shop was on Barkhor Street and was managed by Shao. He was mixed race, half Chinese and half Tibetan, and married to a Lhasa aristocrat. He'd worked with Plum for years, since her Beijing days, and she trusted him. (I didn't get along too well with either Shao or his wife.) Sometimes if I drove Plum to the shop and a consignment of goods from Nepal turned up, I'd help carry stuff in. Or sometimes I'd sit around in the shop for a bit, keeping Plum company. If clients came or Plum and Shao were talking about stuff which had nothing to do with me, I'd go to the Summit Café at the Shangbala Hotel to surf the web and drink fresh-ground imported coffee. I didn't usually go to tea-houses, because Lhasa street gossip didn't interest me. If Plum wanted the car, she'd text me and I'd be back at the shop in two minutes.

Last summer, the Shaos' daughter got into the Tibetan Middle School in Shanghai and her parents organized a going-away party for her in their Xianzu Island villa. Quite a few Lhasa celebs came, and central government officials too, all bringing the traditional red-envelope presents. Present-giving by family and friends was a custom nowadays when kids left for school in China. Plum gave a generous red-envelope present, and she spent hours playing *mahjong* with Mrs Shao as well. We all drank barley liquor and beer. I'd brought my own cup, one I kept for special occasions. We carried on drinking over the evening meal – and that was when Plum noticed I was using my own cup. She looked angry and asked why I'd done that. I said nothing. Surely she must know that old social taboos were making a comeback in Lhasa – the aristocracy still thought lower-class folk were too dirty to share their tableware. She didn't say anything to me for the rest of the evening but, on the way home, she said: 'Isn't your aunt a member of the Neighbourhood Committee? Don't your family have a hardware store?'

'Yes,' I said, 'but my grandfather was only a blacksmith.'

Plum looked pissed off for a good while, then finally burst out with: 'Some revolution! It's bear-faced wickedness!' I'm not sure who she was blaming.

But I liked it that she was so angry for me. If she had asked me then to spend the rest of my life with her, I'd have told her honestly, yes.

We were apart for a long while this time and I really missed her. It had been ages since I'd had a wank but eventually I couldn't hold off any longer. The strange thing was that as soon as I touched myself, all I could think of was my former girlfriends, I couldn't focus on Plum. Were all men unfaithful like that? If wanking was the only time I strayed, did that really count as straying? Anyway, once it was over, I could concentrate on Plum again straightaway.

5

That Tibetan New Year, we were under the 'protection' of the riot police, and we didn't celebrate. We always used to give the house a complete spring-clean and change the rooftop prayer flags on the morning of the third day of the New Year. This year, we did it on the first day and there were no other celebrations. People who went to India in January to join in the Kalachakra Tantra festival were locked up when they got back to Tibet and made to study their 'errors'. Apparently, over 10,000 people were detained, most of them old, because those were the only ones who could get a passport and leave the country. So many people in Lhasa had relatives in detention. Even Party members and retired government cadres, and Mrs Shao's elderly uncle and aunt, were made to attend re-education classes and weren't released till after Serf Emancipation Day at the end of March.

Plum called me at least once a day. She said they weren't selling plane tickets, so she'd have to stay put for the moment.

One day I asked A-Lan, the bookkeeper, if Plum had a Hong Kong ID.

'Yes,' she said.

'Did she have to give up her Beijing residency to get it?'

'No, she's still registered as resident in Beijing.'

I asked if she had a Hong Kong ID and a Beijing resident permit.

'So many questions,' said A-Lan, sounding irritated. 'Yes, that's right. It makes things easier.'

'So she's still got a Beijing resident's permit and a Chinese ID card?' I persisted.

'Of course!'

'Then why can't she buy herself a plane ticket back to Lhasa?'

'Because she's got a lot of work, stupid! And she's been to Burma too. She has several big projects on.'

Plum was treating me like a child. That was the thought that went through my mind, every day from then on, when Plum called.

Then, in the middle of March, Plum said she'd bought me a plane ticket, business class, to Beijing.

I would get to Beijing at last. I was thrilled! She told me to stand outside Arrivals when I got off the plane and she'd pick me up in a white Range Rover.

I spotted the Range Rover, and Plum inside it waving, but she didn't get out to greet me. I'd imagined that, after so long, she'd come to meet me inside the terminal, and we'd throw our arms around each other. Like in the movies.

She let me give her a hug in the car, and smiled. 'Nice car?'

'Very,' I said. It was a Range Rover Aurora, this year's model, three doors, four seats, 4x4, 240 HP, 2-litre, turbocharged, all-aluminium, petrol engine. I'd seen it on the web. It was one fabulous car.

'It's yours,' Plum said. 'I'm going back to Lhasa in it, with you. You can drive it. Do you like it?' I said I did. 'Happy?' she asked.

'Yep.'

Seeing all the skyscrapers on the road from the airport made me feel excited. When Plum finished making her calls, I said: 'Beijing has as many big buildings as Chengdu.'

'Beijing is China's mega-megalopolis, Champie!' she said. 'Isn't it majestic?'

I had no idea what these long words meant but I said: 'Isn't it?'

'You can't just say, "Isn't it?",' she corrected me. '"It is, isn't it?"'

'It is, isn't it?' I repeated.

She'd booked me into a five-star hotel near the Bird's Nest stadium. There was a buffet restaurant where I could help myself to food and drink, and her company would pick up the tab. Tomorrow I could go and visit the Bird's Nest, the Water Cube and the Olympic Park. She had stuff to do today but, tomorrow midday, she'd come and pick me up and I'd start the drive back to Lhasa. She gave me her iPad and told me there was free wifi at the hotel. I said I'd brought my own. 'Give me a kiss then!' she said. We kissed, then, 'Out you get, and take your bag!' and she drove off.

I checked in, had the buffet dinner and drank a bottle of red wine. I went to sleep and, the next morning, had the buffet breakfast, wandered round the Bird's Nest and the Water Cube, and signed the hotel bill . . . and that was pretty much it.

At noon, Plum turned up in the Range Rover. As she got out of the car, I caught sight of her jiggling breasts, and her nice round bottom. She'd changed her mind about driving back with me, just gave me the car, the GPS, map and cash and told me to drive to Golmud. Once I got there, I was to call her. She'd get a plane to Xian then another to Golmud and meet me there. She explained she wanted to try out the land route to Lhasa. 'I got my Beijing driver to run this car in for a month and it can go at high speed now. We'll take the Qinghai–Tibet Highway together to Lhasa, over the roof of the world, past the Kunlun, Hoh Xil and Tanggula mountains. How romantic. It'll be fun, won't it?'

'Yes,' I said.

But I wasn't at all happy, and it wasn't any fun. She'd lied to me about not being allowed to fly back to Lhasa because of her Hong Kong ID. Really, she was just too busy. And this was what she was like when she was busy! She hadn't considered that it was my first ever trip to Beijing. She hadn't spent even a day or two showing me around, entertaining me, taking me to Tian'anmen Square or the Great Wall or a Peking Duck restaurant, and I didn't even have a fuck in a five-star hotel to remember my trip by. And now she wanted me to drive back on my own. What was she talking about, 'majestic' and 'mega-megalopolis'? She'd only got me to Beijing so I could drive her car back to Lhasa.

As soon as I was out of Beijing, the penny dropped. Plum didn't want me hanging around in Beijing. That was why, every time I said I wanted to go with her, she clammed up. Three years we'd been together and she hadn't brought me with her once. And this time, it was only so I could drive her car back. Did she have another man in Beijing? Or was it because she had a lot of friends there and was worried we'd be seen together? But she had scores of friends in Lhasa too, and Lhasa was a lot smaller so it was much harder to avoid bumping into someone we knew. Half of Lhasa knew we were together, but she didn't seem to worry that the news would get back to Beijing.

By the time I got to Golmud, three days later, I'd figured something else out: Plum couldn't be seen trailing a 'Tibetan mastiff puppy' after her. That was why she wanted to keep me at arm's length until we were nearer Tibet. Golmud was part of the Mongolian-Tibetan Autonomous Region so was just about OK, even though its inhabitants were mainly Chinese. Golmud was a transit hub too, and the last city on the Qinghai–Tibet route to have connecting flights from Beijing. That was why Plum had told me to go there. She'd fly there and we'd drive into Tibet together. Once in Tibet, a Chinese businesswoman with a Tibetan driver was no big deal.

But I wasn't just her driver in Lhasa, I was her lover and she was often very affectionate with me in public. So why was she being so careful and over-sensitive and petty-minded in China? I kept going over it in my mind.

I had three days to wait in Golmud before Plum turned up. She first told me two days, but then said she needed an extra day, she had things to do in Beijing.

On the final evening, I was driving along 1st August Road Central, when I spotted some Chinese prostitutes working the Kunlun Park Plaza. One, in particular, was skinny as a rake, and looked like she was on drugs. I couldn't help feeling a bit sorry for her. I did a U-turn and drove back. She was still there. I almost called her over, but then I changed my mind and drove off.

The next day I picked Plum up from the airport. She had a big suitcase with her. We got in the car and kissed, then kissed again. She seemed very relaxed, and kept saying: 'Champie, I've missed you!'

We were going to spend a night in Golmud and head straight for Lhasa the next day. She'd booked another five-star hotel. She checked in and got the bellboy to take her cases up, then she said to me: 'You check out and come back and park here. I'll text you my room number.'

When I got to her room, she had the suitcase open and the table was covered in plastic bags full of food containers. She got one out and announced with a flourish: 'Peking Duck!' Then she got a leather jacket out of the case (another flourish). 'The coolest Harley jacket, made in China, American label, a present for my bad boy Champie!' She helped me into it. 'How does it feel? Do you like it?'

I said yes.

'Happy?'

Yes again.

She caressed me through the jacket then grabbed me. 'Food first or fuck first?'

'Fuck first,' I said.

She pulled me to the bed.

We undressed each other like we'd done so many times before. It was good to have an impromptu pre-dinner fuck. She pushed me into her and cried: 'Yes, yes!' But as soon as I was inside her, my cock wasn't so hard any more. I willed myself to keep going but it was no good. I became panicky. What was going wrong? I shut my eyes and then an image saved me. It was the image of that skinny, junkie slag I'd seen on the street. I imagined stripping off her tight trousers and pushing myself into her. Plum cried out: 'I'm not there yet! Wait for me!' But I'd already shot my load.

'I'm sorry, it's been so long,' I said and she said: 'Don't worry, I had a good time. What a good boy, Champie. You've held on all this time!'

She didn't have a shadow of a doubt.

'Let's do it again tonight.'

'Sure,' I said. 'Of course.'

6

It was just after five in the afternoon and the hotel staff heated up the food Plum had brought from Beijing: Peking duck, shredded pork and eggs, fire-exploded diced chicken in soy paste, and sweet and sour cabbage. We had a meal in our room, keeping the leftovers and sauce in the food containers, and sesame pancakes and nibbles, for the next day on the road.

Then we took the car out for a spin, stopping by a supermarket to get some Kunlun mineral water on the way.

The minutes were ticking by and I was fretting that I wouldn't be able to get it up that night. This was something I'd never imagined. Getting a hard-on when I shouldn't – that happened – but the other way round? I went into the supermarket to buy water and Plum stayed in the car talking on her mobile. There were a couple of girls, Sichuanese probably, in the store. They were plastered with make-up and looked like they were hookers, or maybe bar girls on their way to work. I stared at them and they gave me sidelong glances back. 'Wanna come?' one said, all deadpan. I hesitated, then said 'No.' They gave me dirty looks and went off, making out I'd been wasting their time.

Back in the hotel, Plum went into the bathroom to take off her make-up and brush her teeth. 'Let's have an early night,' she said. I thought she was letting me off the hook, I could see she was tired. But, next thing I know, she's lying on the bed: 'Come here, Champie.'

Last night's skinny Chinese junkie got me hard enough to come in the afternoon, but she wasn't having any effect tonight. The two girls I'd seen in the supermarket were trashy and I found their faces and bodies repellent, but now they were all I had to call on.

Thankfully, Plum came pretty quickly and then turned over and worked on me. Then she wiped her hands, chucked the tissues on the floor and snuggled down under the duvet. 'The alarm's set for four a.m.,' she said. 'I'm dead tired, absolutely bushed.' And soon she was snoring.

I didn't sleep well. Things were bugging me, and I tossed and turned. My little guy wouldn't obey orders. I had disappointed myself. I was worried this might be long-term. I never imagined that one day I'd need to fantasize about a prostitute to get it up with a woman in bed.

I looked at Plum, snoring by my side. I wanted to stay with this woman but I didn't fancy her any more. I could delude myself about my feelings but there was no mistaking this message from the little guy: Plum just didn't get my tantric juices going now.

And if I really didn't fancy Plum any more, what was I going to do? How would I get by?

I liked the life I was living now. I'd acquired a taste for the good life. Plum had been very generous with her gifts. She bought my food, drink and clothes. I had absolutely nothing to complain about. The truth was I couldn't do without her.

In fact, I had a much better life in Lhasa than her driver did in Beijing. But of course I wasn't just her driver, I was her man. Her 'blood's sicker than water' man.

It was true she could be really annoying, like bringing me to Beijing for work but making it sound like she was inviting me there to see the sights. Every step of the way she'd set it up entirely to suit herself, though she kept asking me: 'Are you enjoying it? Having fun?' I hadn't enjoyed it or had fun, not at all, OK?

It must be because things hadn't worked out in Beijing. Everything would be better again once we were back in Lhasa. I'd fancy Plum again, just like normal. We just needed to get back to Lhasa.

7

The guesthouses between Golmud and Lhasa were crap so we decided to head straight for Lhasa and not stop on the way. I had a gut feeling that we needed to get back quickly. Then things would be OK again.

It was going to take us fifteen hours or more to make the journey, depending on the state of the road. There were speed restrictions now between Amdo and Lhasa so I guessed we wouldn't be home till very late. But I had stamina, so that didn't worry me. I knew I could do it.

We'd planned to set off before dawn, but when we woke up and looked out of the window, it looked too cold so we went back to bed for another hour or so. We got up at six and Plum wanted a hot drink before we left. We boiled some water in our room, and mixed it with some black sesame paste, but that just made us hungrier so we made our way down to the restaurant for breakfast. In the end it was after seven before we left. We got to the Nanshankou checkpoint and had to queue up behind a bunch of lorries. Then we went to fill up with petrol.

I really wanted to hit the road. I knew this stretch. I wasn't bothered about the weather even though it was unpredictable in March and April, swinging from sunshine to rain, snow or hail, just like that. It was too bad, though, that after the Naij Tal army post, we hit a convoy of Lanzhou Military Region trucks, all of them with L-plates on them, rookie army drivers under instruction and driving really slowly. Plum told me not to worry but when she woke up after a nap and found we were still behind those trucks, she began to get fed up. Actually, I'd managed to squeeze past dozens of them while she was asleep, but there were many more ahead of us still.

Finally we got to the Xidatan army post and the trucks all drove into camp. Of course we didn't stop for a break, just carried on and put as much distance between them and us as we could so as to make up a bit of time. 'Let's have something to eat,' said Plum, but I suggested getting past Hoh Xil first. Every now and then, Plum put a morsel into my mouth, and something into her own, and it sort of filled us up. Then she switched on the wireless router, got online on her iPhone and didn't say another word, not even about needing a roadside pee.

The road to Wudaoliang was quite flat. There was a local saying, 'Kokonor women don't take baths, Kokonor mountains don't grow grass.' There certainly wasn't much to look at, the weather was good, there was little traffic and I could put my foot down. Plum listened to her Faye Wong and Dadawa songs over and over, till she fell asleep again. I wanted to get past the Tanggula range in daylight and then stop for a proper meal in Amdo. At least if we could get to Yanshiping and have something to eat and drink and . . . I was startled by furious hooting and wrenched the steering wheel back to my side of the road just as a pick-up truck coming in the opposite direction roared past on my left. I slowed down and stopped by the roadside. I looked at Plum, who was still napping. I'd just nodded off too.

The air was thin up here. Was I short of oxygen, or short of sleep?

I didn't dare drive on, so I pulled further into the side and cut the engine, then took a nap.

A little later, I felt Plum give me a prod. 'Let me drive for a bit,' she said. I didn't bother protesting, and we swapped over and I carried on napping.

Just half an hour later and I was back to my normal self again. I didn't know how I'd managed to fall asleep at the wheel. I'd never done that before, even when I hadn't slept for nights.

When we got to the River Marchu, we swapped back again.

From Yanshiping, the first town in Tibet, to Lhasa, there were six checkpoints on route 109, every one of them manned by rookie Tibetan cops or armed police who went through our documents and bags with a fine-tooth comb, making damn sure that no Tibetan who wasn't a resident got into Lhasa.

Why weren't Tibetans from outside Lhasa allowed into the city? After all, they were Tibetans, weren't they?

There were a lot of things bugging me that day but I didn't let on.

Plum had a headache from the altitude and didn't feel like getting out of the car at the checkpoint. She told me to take her Beijing ID and go through. She'd completely forgotten she'd told me earlier she only had a Hong Kong returnee's permit and couldn't get back to Lhasa.

Every stage along the route, the police gave you a card to get stamped at the next stage. You couldn't take too long or do the stage too fast either. At two stages, I got there too early because I'd been speeding. The first time, I got fined 200 *yuan*, but the second time, the young Tibetan cop let me off. It was two in the morning before we got back to Lhasa.

One good thing was that we were too tired for anything except sleep. That was one more night over.

And tomorrow?

8

What could go wrong now I was back in Lhasa? I was back to the life I knew so well, and back to my old self, the super-fit man who was absolutely normal in the head. Of course there was nothing wrong with me. Are you kidding? I was a tough guy, a Tibetan mastiff, a heart throb. I remembered the slogan we learned in Mandarin classes when I was little: 'Onward and upward.'

I got up in the morning and left Plum sleeping. I washed both 4x4s, the Range Rover and the Toyota. A new day had begun.

Plum chose to ride in the Range Rover with me this morning, and that was a big boost for my status. We went to the shop and, as I drew up in the courtyard, everyone – Shao and all the employees – came out to welcome Plum back and admire the new car. It was a three-door, for two people. That made us a couple, not boss and driver. Plum and I got in and out of it together and rode around in it, and that told the rest of the world that our relationship was out in the open. I felt that even Shao, who was a sly man, treated me with a friendliness he'd never done before. Everyone looked envious. I'd gone up in the world.

So why wasn't I happier? In everyone else's eyes we were a proper couple now, so why did I feel so down? I remembered what Shao said, that the higher up you go in the job, the greater the pressure, and more rights meant more responsibility and so on. Maybe that was it. I sneaked a look at Shao. The hypocritical bastard had lost his friendly look. In fact, he seemed to be waiting to see what games I'd play next. He had a know-it-all look on his face, the wily old so-and-so. Did he guess something was up with me?

But he couldn't possibly know. So what was I panicking about? Not being up to the job? But I had no reason to worry. I had every confidence in the little guy, he wasn't going to let me down. Ever since he'd stood up all of a sudden when I was ten years old, he'd never let me down. All these years, we'd chased girls together and we got on really well, and I'd given him lots of good times. I mustn't keep thinking about it, I really mustn't. All this thinking was getting me down. If I just stopped thinking, I'd be fine.

To be on the safe side, I went online and looked at some porn, just to get those tantric juices flowing.

Plum finished her meeting with Shao and the bookkeeper, A-Lan, just after four o'clock and came out in a very good mood. We got in the car. 'Where to?' I asked.

'To Mr Ouyang's,' she said. 'Then you can go home and have something to eat. You don't need to wait for me.'

She hadn't invited me to go along with her to Mr Ouyang's place.

She'd told me not to wait up. But I'd always waited up for her before. I'd never gone to sleep before she was asleep, and I'd certainly never let her find me asleep in her bed when she came home. That, to me, was just the right way to behave. But today it suddenly occurred to me that if she got back and I was asleep then I wouldn't need to have sex with her. I lay in bed but I just didn't feel sleepy. I was a lousy good-for-nothing with a guilty conscience. I got up again and pulled on my jeans. I would wait up for her. I wanted to believe in myself.

I watched some porn DVDs and listened for the door. Finally, in the small hours, Ouyang's driver brought Plum home. She never called me to collect her. She was in a very good mood and pretty tipsy too. She was delighted when she saw I was still up, dumped her bag, shoes and some folders down and said: 'We have nothing on tomorrow morning.' Then she gave me a couple of winks and that special look.

I seized her in my arms and got her to the bed, keen to show my eagerness. We each got undressed. I was at half-mast. Here I was back in Lhasa, and still impotent. I shut my eyes and conjured up the starlets of the porn film I'd been watching but it was no good. I searched my memory for the last girls who'd made an impression on me, the junkie prostitute, some Sichuanese girls, even A-Lan the bookkeeper, but none of them worked. I was in despair. I reached inside her and rubbed her G-spot hard but she didn't come. She just gasped and cried: 'Champie, cock, cock, gimme cock!'

She tried to reach back with her left hand and grab me but I wouldn't let her. Her big round arse bucked and reared and suddenly I was hard. Without a second's thought, I pushed myself into her arse. She shrieked, and tried to struggle free but I gripped her violently from behind and wouldn't let her go. I had her completely immobilized. 'A-ya! A-ya!' she was shrieking, but she had to let me do it anyway.

Afterwards she got up, not looking at me, and hopped barefoot to the bathroom, the condom wedged between her buttocks. I heard the sound of her peeing, then there were some farts, then plopping and more tinkling. Then she washed between her legs.

I couldn't believe what I'd done. It was the first time I'd done that with a girl. Of course I hadn't fucked a man like that either, or been fucked, either. That just wasn't my thing.

She came out of the bathroom. 'I didn't like that, Champie! I really didn't.' She seemed to be walking with difficulty. She went to the mirror and looked at her behind, turning this way and that, then pulled a tissue from the box and pressed it into her. 'It's all torn,' she said. She went back to the bathroom and applied some cream, then came and lay down on the bed. 'I didn't like it when you did that,' she said emphatically. Then she rolled over heavily and settled down to sleep.

The next morning, she was awake early and sat up in bed. Then she seemed to remember that she was in pain, and hobbled into the bathroom. I'd been awake for a while, and was lying there thinking, but I got up when she did. The whole morning she was busy reading the project files she'd brought back the night before, making notes on them. She was in a good mood, full of fighting spirit and looked ready to do a major deal in the afternoon. I made her a bowl of noodles at midday. As she ate them she gave me a proper telling-off: 'I didn't like what you did last night, Champie, you hurt me. You know I'm scared of pain. Don't ever do it again. Call me conservative if you like, but I don't think it's fun at all. You know what makes me angriest? It's that you went right against our pact that we'd always be willing partners. You're just self-obsessed.'

And I knew I'd never repeat this kind of 'spurt of the moment' activity either.

9

After lunch, Plum went to the Tibet Autonomous Region government offices for a meeting. She told me to take her in the Toyota and she sat in the back. I'd gone back to being her driver.

We drove in through the compound gate, and Mr Ouyang's car pulled in behind us. The two of them went inside, looking like they had something up their sleeves. Zhang, Ouyang's driver, called out 'Hi!', obviously thinking we'd go and find parking spaces together, but I drove out of the compound and back along the road. It wasn't that I thought I was too good to mix with the drivers, it was that I had something to do and only a short time to do it in. I had to prepare myself to serve Plum tonight.

Down Jinzhu West Road in the direction of Xuexin Village there was a 'club' where, a few years back, I went with some Chinese who'd employed me to drive them around. The club gave me a VIP membership card. I'd driven past many times since then so I knew they were still in business. I got myself a room now and, quick as I could, chose a petite Chinese girl and took her up to my room. I reckoned Plum would be in the meeting for an hour so I'd have just enough time.

I didn't bother asking the girl's name, just told her to take her clothes off, every stitch. I felt myself begin to swell. That meant I could believe in myself again.

Once she'd stripped off, I made her lie down on the bed. Too bad she'd had a boob job so they didn't flop naturally but stood up when she was lying down. But what made me excited and relieved was that I was still hard.

I told the girl I wanted to watch her touch herself and if she satisfied me I'd give her more money as a reward. She seemed quite happy to do that and started to caress herself and moan. I told her not to touch her breasts, just down below, and she obeyed. I had to remember her caresses, her expression, her cries of pleasure, I had to stay hungry, my tantric juices had to boil, and I had to save it all up for Plum.

She gave a poor imitation of an orgasm, it was so fake she obviously wasn't trying very hard, but I was still super hard and a couple of times I so nearly came I had to look at the ceiling and think of something else.

The girl asked if I wanted her to make me come but I shook my head. She was quite friendly and offered to do 'fire and ice': she'd take me in her warm mouth and then cool it with a cold wet towel. She made her mouth into an O-shape and giggled as she told me I could come in her mouth. Come in her mouth? Ever since the time I'd gone out with a couple of my bosses and we had some Chinese hookers, I'd been keen on blow-jobs.

I forced myself to say: 'No, forget it.' She never knew how hard it was for me to control myself.

I looked at my watch. It was time to go, but I was still like a rod of iron. I ordered the little guy to go soft but he put up a fight and just wouldn't bow his head. This kind of disobedience only happened to you when you were eleven or twelve years old, when it somehow grew during class, till you got worried about the end-of-class bell. Sometimes, if it refused to go down in time you just had to waddle out of the classroom with it sticking up in front of you, and no time to worry whether anyone was looking or not.

I waited a minute or two. Annoyingly, just at that moment, Plum called to ask where I was. I lied and said I'd gone to fill up with petrol and could be there in five minutes, and she said not to worry, she'd get a lift with Mr Ouyang and I should go straight to his restaurant on Xianzu Island.

I looked at my watch again. Plum had only been in her meeting for forty-five minutes. I looked at myself. It had finally gone down a bit.

10

When I got to Ouyang's posh restaurant, the waitress recognized me and took me to the side room. I pushed the door ajar and saw Plum, Ouyang and a few of the senior execs from his company drinking toasts. It seemed like they were celebrating something. Plum saw me and came over. 'You sit in the main restaurant,' she said cheerfully. 'Have whatever you want to eat and drink.'

I took her at her word, and ordered some bottles of Belgian beer and a bottle of Chilean red. I took a seat in the corner and started drinking. I wasn't bothered about having to drive afterwards. This was Lhasa, after all, what was there to worry about? Shao, the shop manager, came in. He must have seen me but he didn't look at me or say 'Hi!', just went straight into the side room. It was uproar in there, they must have done a very big deal at the meeting.

Their meal went on for a long time, from five in the afternoon until the early hours. They spent their time talking, I spent it playing games on my iPhone.

When we got home, Plum wanted sex of course, but that was fine, I'd primed myself that afternoon. I got on top of her and thought of the girl at the club and it was like an engine had fired up between my legs. Plum didn't even have time to gasp: 'Don't come! Wait for me!' Afterwards, she didn't say anything, just went to the bathroom, then came back to bed, put her head down and went to sleep.

Things must have been going really well for her because her mind was constantly on her business deals. That meant that, for the moment, she was too busy to think about what was going on with us. But one day it would occur to her that there was something about my performance that just wasn't right. Unless I could improve my performance pretty quickly, it wouldn't take her long to tally up the fucks and she wouldn't be accusing me just of being self-obsessed. Didn't they say Chinese people were naturally suspicious? With her intelligence, she'd certainly suspect that I'd lost interest in her or even got myself another girl. She was right too. To have sex with Plum now, I had to have another girl in my head. And it had to be a different sex object every time.

Of course I'd heard about men and women having affairs outside marriage and fantasizing about their lovers when they were making love with their spouses, or even shouting their lover's name. A driver I knew once told me that he could only do it with his wife by putting a nude photo of a foreign woman over his wife's face. I'd had plenty of sexual experience. I knew having sex with one woman while thinking of another was pretty common, and understandable. But this was something else. Every time I was screwing Plum, I had to think about a different girl. There was no way I could recycle the same image, and I couldn't depend on porn films to get me going either. It had to be a girl I'd just seen. This was really scary, and I was terrified. How long could we go on like this?

Of course you could say this was just my latest nightmare and – who knows – everything might go back to normal after a bit. But how long would it take? Judging by the last few days, I couldn't kid myself it would all be all right tomorrow.

The key thing was that I had to prove my loyalty to her every day. And it wouldn't just be paying lip service to my duties. Every day it had to be the real McCoy, a real, physical labour of love. There was no way I could fake it for Plum. Any day now, I might not find my sex object, and then I wouldn't be able to perform. After a couple of times of this happening, my cover would be blown and I'd be in trouble.

I suddenly wanted to walk away from it and let it all go, just to avoid the moment when Plum would finally catch me, do the fuck tally and interrogate me. She wouldn't let me off the hook until I fessed up either. Just the thought was unbearable. I had no idea how to explain it, and anyway, it would be so hurtful to her. I didn't want to hurt Plum and I didn't have the heart to tell her the truth. Because it wasn't her who had changed, it was me.

I thought back to the beginning. It really had been a case of 'act in haste, repent at leisure'. First, I'd got horny for her, then she'd seduced me. We'd both been willing partners then. Who would have imagined what was happening now? I so wished I was still just Plum's driver. As a boss, she was really decent. But would she let me go back to how things were? I didn't think so. You can't turn the clock back. I could go and find another employer to drive for, but I couldn't stay with her and just be her driver and water her plants without giving her sexual services.

If I didn't make love with Plum, I would lose everything.

But my little guy was telling me in no uncertain terms that it wasn't on.

My little guy was forcing the big guy's hand. I had to decide. I knew the options: either I left Plum straightaway or I had to find a new sex object every day to keep the sexual services going strong. Every day? That would be exhausting, not to mention challenging, technically speaking. What if I miscalculated, ran out of juice and forgot to recharge the batteries, and the little guy went on go-slow or crashed altogether? I just couldn't do it. Unless a miracle happened and a reliable sex object appeared, one I could use and reuse in my fantasies.

11

Every day, the Lhasa sun shone brilliantly but I was plunged deep in gloom. I thought I'd go and get an eyeful of some young foreign female tourists. The early tour groups normally turned up on the first of April every year. But at the Lingtsang Boutique Hotel I'd only seen a few old folks, so I went off to the Shangbala Hotel instead, hoping there wouldn't just be those giant German or Scandinavian females, striding around looking intrepid in their thick waterproofs, climbing boots and gigantic backpacks. I'd got women who were taller and chunkier than me into bed in the past when there was nothing to stop me doing that, but that was not what I had in mind today. I realized that what I really wanted was a petite girl. Since I'd had problems getting it up, I had no appetite for the big ones any more, just the little ones. I'd never been particularly picky about women, maybe I'd been too generous in fact. All shapes and sizes could get me going. But things had changed. My sexual tastes had narrowed down to just one type – a petite girl. The realization scared me, really scared me. The more selective my tastes got, the narrower the field and the smaller the odds of finding a sex object.

The strangest thing was that there were no foreign tour groups at the Shangbala Hotel today. In the Summit Café, there was only one foreign woman, and she was getting on a bit. I'd seen her face before. She was one of the few foreigners who had a permit to work in Lhasa at the moment.

I stood looking down Danjielin Road. Where were those petite young foreign girls hiding themselves?

I was a bit worried. Plum might call at any moment and ask me to take her somewhere and that would be the end of my free time. I needed to make the most of this morning, when she was at the shop, to find today's sex object somewhere around Barkhor Street.

I once saw a porn film called *The Hunter*. I've forgotten what it was about but I felt like the hunter now, searching every nook and cranny for sexual inspiration. I could only use Chinese girls once, but maybe the foreign ones could be used a few times. If so, how many? Even if they couldn't, that wasn't too bad. The Lhasa tourist season was about to start and, so long as there weren't any political incidents, there would be a steady stream of tour groups turning up and I didn't need to worry about finding foreign girls. If they did impose restrictions on foreign tour groups . . . well, no need to go there yet. But the mind plays strange tricks. I was becoming obsessed with the idea that my quarry had to be petite. I wandered along Barkhor Street, getting frantic as I hunted for that elusive sex object.

But the season hadn't started properly yet. It was still chilly at the beginning of April and there were no petite foreign girls strolling around.

I'd got as far as the Jokhang Temple, and was standing by the wall between the World Heritage sign and the ticket office when I saw a young girl among a crowd of women prostrating themselves on the ground in reverence. From her clothes I guessed she was from the Ü-Tsang region. She was tiny. She was prostrating herself like the others and, from behind, she seemed like my perfect fantasy woman. And not even foreign, I thought to myself. My little guy retorted: 'Idiot! Who said she has to be foreign?'

'Cut it out,' I protested. 'It isn't proper, leave her alone, she's saying her prayers.'

Well, that may have been what the big guy thought, but the little guy kept talking: 'That's her! That's her!' And next thing I know he's slowly pulling me over to take a look. I went close and craned my neck so I could just about see her face, then I walked away. I'd go and find a foreign girl, there were bound to be some around hotels like the Yabshi Phunkhang, the Kyichu, the Yak or the Banak Shol.

I turned out of Barkhor Street but I hadn't gone far when armed police stopped me to check my ID. They'd already done that on my way in. How many times in a day were they going to do it? Once they finished their checks, I wandered around aimlessly, and finally found myself at the Lutsang where I got myself something I hadn't had in years: a glass of sweet tea. Around me, men sat gossiping, no doubt with informers eavesdropping, about anything from world events to what utterances the Dalai Lama had made recently and who had been roped into political 'study sessions'. But none of it had anything to do with me. You can't carry on like this, can you? I said to myself. Just getting by, day by day, what kind of a life was that for anyone? I knocked my head on the table. You fucking stupid cock, stop messing with me. Then I headed back to the shop in a very bad mood.

It was obvious when I got there that things weren't going to get any better today. A consignment of goods had arrived from Nepal, and I was supposed to help unload and make an inventory as I did so. Plum told me to shut the front door in case we got people wandering in. The shop hardly ever got passing trade. We were selling fine goods at high prices, and most clients came because they'd been introduced by people we already knew. For Plum, the shop was just a convenient depot for the goods and a place to meet clients, and it was obvious from the frontage that her business didn't depend on it. Today's consignment included Nepalese Buddhist statuettes, *thangkas* and other sacred objects, as well as some genuine antique statuettes she'd picked up somewhere. Most of them would be sold on to outlets around China.

Jigme was the shop's expert repairer of statuettes and *thangkas*. A-Lan was the bookkeeper and in charge of stocks. Shao, the shop manager, normally took care of sales. Shao was so smarmy I couldn't stand him but he only had to open his mouth and speak English and foreigners were eating out of his hand. Today he and Plum were closeted in his office in discussions, leaving Jigme, A-Lan and me to do odd jobs around the shop. Plum didn't like having too many employees, she always said an extra worker was an extra headache. She liked to have a pared-down workforce, and everyone had to be able to turn their hand to different tasks and be willing partners. That way all her people could earn a bit more money. If we stuck close to the mother tiger, she'd always provide. The thing she most hated was her people leaving her. We were her family, she used to say, one big Chinese family, and blood was sicker than water.

I let Shao's wife in. She looked right through me and didn't say 'Hi!' Once, when I took Plum to the Shaos, the woman had caught me using one of their cups to get myself some water, and had a go at me. She told me to bring my own cup next time.

I reckon she suspected Shao of getting a leg-over with his boss. Hah! She can't have liked that. But today she'd come to attend the meeting, no doubt because she could pull strings with some of her fancy relatives. The old nobility of Lhasa.

I got on pretty well with A-Lan. She was friendly and I was happy to carry the boxes in for her. But she and Mrs Shao were both ugly as sin, and as far as getting my tantric juices going, they were useless. In fact, if the little guy was hard, just the thought of them made him go soft and I didn't feel like a man any more. That was too bad. I had a deadline to meet – tonight.

12

'Champie,' Plum asked me, 'what you think of this statuette?'

She wouldn't normally ask me a question like that. I wasn't an expert in sacred objects. In fact, I'd never been good at any of my studies. My granddad's generation went off with the Communist Party and my parents, when they were alive, always said the Party was their religion. Only my grandma was a believer, and she only started going to the temple again after I was born, or so the family said. When I was acting as driver and guide, I could bluff it by making the odd pronouncement about the Buddhist Canon of Iconography and other such rigmarole. That would get me by with bog-standard tourists, but with the real experts like Plum, Shao and Jigme, I never dared open my mouth.

Plum had taken the statuette of the White Tara Bodhisattva from the shop. Back home, she unwrapped it from the silk *khata* and displayed it on a table against the wall. She arranged a ceiling light over it, then called me to come and look. I peered at it from all sides and said something like: 'Nice handiwork.'

'Any different from the other Taras in the shop, do you think?' she asked.

Nothing scared me more than being questioned like this. I did think the statuette was a bit different but couldn't express it in words and didn't want to put my foot in it, so I just said no. But that wasn't good enough for Plum. 'Look a bit closer, at the face,' she insisted.

'I can't see anything different.'

'Don't you think the face is like me?' she asked.

I didn't think so, but said: 'Maybe, a little bit.'

'It's just like me when I was young,' Plum went on. 'When I was at middle school.'

Well, you must have had a facelift since then, I thought to myself. Of course I didn't say that.

'It's all my fault,' she went on. 'The original Tara statuettes were fine as they were and I made a lot of money from them. Why did I have to go and change them? But I suddenly thought the Nepali Taras were a bit crude so I got one remodelled. It looked all right in the picture and I didn't think it looked like me. The face is beautiful, of course, but the clients might be put off and think it's too Chinese. I need to give it some thought. Perhaps we shouldn't get too many made. It might be safer to stick to the Nepali models we had before. The good thing is I only got one sample, so I'll keep it at home and enjoy it.'

If only I hadn't felt like I was going to the gallows tonight I might have teased Plum for being self-obsessed and behaving like those Chinese tantric devotees who fantasize that they're heavenly groupies.

Plum went into the bedroom and I looked more closely at the figurine. The face seemed thinner than the usual Tara Bodhisattva faces but that meant it was even less like Plum's chubby, round features.

The Tara's face was quite serene, exactly like the ones in the shop, and very pretty.

The eyes gleamed, so she looked more expressive than most, but that was the only difference.

Apart from the breasts. These were a bit smaller and higher, not full and round but pointy, a bit like missiles, very sweet. Maybe Plum had had pointy, perky breasts at middle school and they'd only become full and round later on. I cheered up. She had only made me look at the face, not the torso, otherwise I would have seen the difference because I was an expert at female breasts. But now that I had, would I dare tease Plum today? That might be a step too far.

But gawping at the Tara couldn't save me, even though I stood there for a while. Plum had changed into a loose robe and was standing in the bedroom doorway hissing like a snake. I turned to her and she winked a couple of times and gave me a naughty look. I knew that expression so well.

Then lightning struck. Wasn't that the expression on the face of the Tara? The statuette had been modelled on Plum's wink, with the slight lift of her eyelids and that gleam in her eye, hadn't it?

I seemed to me the Tara gave me a couple of winks.

I felt the wind blowing through the prayer flags. I followed Plum into the bedroom. I wasn't going to the gallows after all, I was flying high.

I gently took Plum's clothes off and kneaded and licked all the most sensitive spots on her body. Underneath me, she was digging her long fingernails into me, first my back, then my buttocks. I was driving her wild, almost letting her come, then stopping her again. Then – just at the instant when that growl started deep in her throat – I shut my eyes and imagined the Tara turning into a great ball of light and dissolving into me.

We pulled apart and collapsed in a daze on the bed, breathing heavily.

'Champie, you're a sex fiend,' she said.

PART TWO

Straw Dogs

Chapter Two

1

I NEVER GET into fights. Haven't done that for years. Until the other day, that is, when I got into a fight with some Chinese 'releasing living creatures' into the river.

Mind you, I've nothing against releasing living creatures as a way of earning merit. It's part of our religion. Sure, I eat animal flesh; in fact, I love any kind of fresh meat, beef and mutton from Lhasa's Muslim butchers, chicken, duck and pork trucked into Tibet, you name it. I'm not keen on sea fish, though I'll eat it. Many Tibetans don't eat fish and shellfish. They reckon they should only kill those creatures that they really need to eat. In my case, I just don't like the taste. Once I went on a trip to Guizhou province with some Chinese friends, and we tried dog meat. But that was just a one-off, I'm not in the habit of eating dog. Anyway, I eat meat so I can't object when people kill animals for me to eat. But I've no objection to devotees releasing living creatures either.

When I was a kid, I used to play in the Lhasa River with my friends. Devotees would release their fish and we'd wait downstream and catch them and sell them back to the people they'd bought them from. Once I saw someone release a lizard into the water. It started paddling frantically because it could see that a bunch of toads on the riverbank were coming after it. That was one of my scariest childhood memories. Later on, I heard people say that you should take care what you released and where, otherwise you were just sentencing the creature to death.

Anyway, that day, Plum was out of town and I was feeling bored. I was mooching along the riverbank, thinking about this and that, for example, Plum and the Tara. A few weeks had passed but one thing hadn't changed: when I fucked Plum, all I could think of was the Tara statuette. Before that, all my fantasies had been about women you had sex with once and then forgot, a different one every time, but now it was the Tara or nothing. I couldn't get it up for Plum any more, only for the Bodhisattva. I had to imagine I was having sex with a goddess just so I could make Plum believe it was all for her. And the strange thing about it was that the Tara could get me hard not once, not twice, but as many times as I wanted, for as long as I wanted. She granted my every wish. It was like snow melt on the sacred mountain – the more you drank, the more there was left. Plum said my performance in bed was getting better and better. She was super-happy with me.

All that worked fine so long as lust and love stayed separate, and the little guy and the big guy each did their own thing.

In fact, now that I had the Tara to fantasize about, I could stick around with Plum long-term.

So why was I feeling so pissed off? The trouble was I didn't like what I was doing, I really didn't. I was deceiving Plum and offending the Tara. On the surface, I was living the good life, but inside I felt like I was condemned to wander for ever in the lower realms of *samsara*. I was doing wrong. If there was a hell, I was on my way there, and if there was a next life, I'd be reborn as a hungry ghost or a beast. If you sinned, there would always be payback time. Even though I didn't believe in *karma*, or anything at all, I still felt I'd fallen in the gutter and was covered in filth.

I'd forgotten that around the time of the Buddha's birthday, many people would be releasing fish and other creatures. I saw a cheerful crowd of men and women pouring out of tour buses.

Three of the men were each carrying a big basin with a turtle in it. The turtles had ridged shells, and they were bigger than Indian chapattis. What with their long tails too, they were ferocious-looking beasts. They obviously weren't Tibetan turtles. 'What are those?' I asked. One of the men told me they were American snapping turtles. I thought of the Chinese rats which had driven little Tibetan rats to extinction, and reacted instinctively: 'You can't release them here!' I didn't say why, just tried to stop them. I grabbed them and cuffed them a bit, not too hard, but someone called the police and we all got carted off to the police station.

There were a lot of them and they all said I'd started it, which might have been true. I wasn't worried. I knew Plum would send someone along to get me out. That little fisticuffs really perked me up and in my mind I went over the moves I'd made and the punches I'd landed. Anyway, it wasn't long before Shao turned up and they let me go. He didn't say much, just that Plum had come back today, and wanted me to go to the hospital for a check-up and to get a doctor's note. So long as my injuries weren't serious, I was to join them for dinner at Mr Ouyang's restaurant and we'd talk about how to deal with the incident.

It turned out that the men I'd got into a fight with were in Lhasa on business. Maybe they'd been told by some fortune-teller to go and buy turtles and release them, and they'd forked out on some big snapper turtles. Releasing them was their way of praying for good luck. Not surprising they didn't want me butting in. The business world being small, we could probably find some common acquaintances.

'So it's not a big problem, then?' asked Plum.

'No,' said Mr Ouyang. 'The police won't touch a fight between a Tibetan and Chinese. They'd rather both sides settled it between themselves.'

'And Champie did nothing wrong.' Plum defended me.

I heard afterwards that they released the snapper turtles into the river anyway. And honestly, I really didn't give a toss about snapper turtles, fish or even shrimps. I wasn't the Goddess of Mercy. I was just venting my frustrations and those men happened to be in the way.

2

When I woke up the next morning, I'd thought of a reason for leaving Plum. How about if I said I'd fallen for another girl? That I was prepared to give up everything for love? I mean, didn't they say: 'All's fair in love and war'? It sounded good. I liked it; at least, I liked it better than saying I couldn't get it up any more. Of course, Plum would be upset, she hated people leaving her, and she had no idea it was all I thought about every day. But wouldn't she be even more upset if I was completely honest and said I was leaving her because she didn't do anything for me any more so I wanted out? Whatever I said, she'd be devastated. I just couldn't make up my mind which would be the least hurtful.

When I drove Plum to the shop in the morning, A-Lan told me to go and meet some people off the plane. She handed me two placards. One had three names written on it: the general secretary and two managers from the NFMIA, the Non-Ferrous Metals Industries Association. The second had only one name: 'Shell'. I could tell how important people were from how we picked them up at the airport. If they were really important, Plum would come with me in the car. Really, really important, and she might even borrow Shao's Audi and go and pick them up herself and leave me behind. If they weren't important, they had to make their own way. Today's three were only middling important, and the fact that I was to meet two groups in one trip put them down another notch. But collecting and delivering people was what I did, so I was going to do a good job anyhow.

I folded down one of the seats in the back row, leaving just the one seat up. That was the way the Land Cruiser was designed, it made more luggage space. That way, you could have one person sitting in the back, two in the middle row, and one in the front passenger seat, all nice and comfortable for four passengers.

Shell was the first one out of Arrivals. She had no suitcase, just a rucksack. She walked up and stood in front of me. 'Shell?' I asked. She said nothing, just raised one hand in a perfunctory greeting. 'Would you mind having a seat for a few moments?' I said. 'The others aren't out yet.' She still said nothing, just moved a couple of paces away and stood motionless, not even looking around her.

She was clearly a girl not a boy, in spite of the short hair, tight-fit black leather jacket, red scarf, narrow-cut jeans and oversized hiking boots. She was very pale, and had dark-rimmed eyes in a long thin face. I thought she looked like a skinny version of an Angry Bird.

Then the general secretary and the two managers came out. They must have been desperate for a smoke, because the first thing they did was light up. I pushed the luggage trolley and led Shell and the three men to the Toyota. I had just opened the boot to put the bags in, when Shell, still without a word, opened the front door and got into the passenger seat. I was on the point of asking her to sit at the back as she was the smallest, but now that she'd seated herself, I could hardly ask her to move. The managers dithered a moment, then the one who was slightly younger, but bigger, threw his cigarette on the ground and squeezed himself into the back seat.

We hadn't been driving long when the three men lit up again. Shell turned and said, rather formally: 'Please would you mind not smoking, gentlemen?' Then she paused, and added: 'I don't want to breathe in your smoke.' I saw the men's reaction in the rear-view mirror – they were first gobsmacked, then mortified. 'And it'll give us altitude sickness too,' she continued, still looking at them. The general secretary hesitated a moment, then stubbed his cigarette out. The other two followed suit. 'Thank you,' said Shell, and faced forward again, without another word.

We were entering Lhasa when I heard the senior man say quietly to his companions: 'I don't feel well. How about you?' The young man at the back said he didn't either. And the third: 'I feel a bit odd too.'

'I'll give the hotel a ring,' I said, 'and ask them to get the oxygen bags and wheelchairs ready for you.' But the general secretary demurred, saying there was no need.

In fact, they were just a bit queasy. Some oxygen would fix that. After I'd delivered them to the hotel, I got back in the car and said to Shell: 'Are you OK?' She didn't look at me, just gave a slight nod. 'Where would you like me to take you?' I asked.

'What did my mum say?'

I had no idea who her mother was . . . Plum? A-Lan? I hazarded a guess. 'Er, Plum didn't say.'

'Is there anyone at home?' Shell asked without looking at me.

'No, not at the moment, but I can let you in if you like. Why not go there and put your feet up?'

She nodded again, still without looking at me.

When we got to the house she turned and thanked me. 'There are things to eat, and drinks, in the kitchen,' I told her, but she just stood there saying nothing. 'It's all there, in the kitchen. Make yourself at home.' Still no response. 'If you need anything, just ring my mobile,' I tried again. She got her mobile out and looked at me. I told her the number and she drop-called it. 'Just call if you need anything. My name's Champa. You have a rest now.' She nodded. 'Just have a rest,' I repeated, flustered. Then I left.

I drove back to the shop.

'Where's Shell?' Plum asked when she saw me.

At home, I told her.

'Why did you take her there?' she exclaimed. 'I booked her a room at the Lingtsang Boutique Hotel!'

'You didn't tell me that.'

'I didn't tell you because I asked you to drive her here first. I mean, that's where I am, so of course, you should have brought her here first. If you didn't know, you could have called and asked.'

I couldn't argue with that, it was just that there was something about Shell that made me forget all about phoning Plum, and I'd decided, off my own bat, to take her to Plum's house. 'I'll go and get her then,' I said. Plum thought for a moment. 'No, don't bother. I've almost finished here. I'll go straight home, and you can take her to the hotel this evening.'

Plum and Shao soon finished their meeting. Plum got in the car with me and Shao took the NFMIA people to lunch.

When we got back, we found the front door ajar, a chair propping it open. Shell was crouched by the kennel where the compound's two guard dogs were kept, playing with them. When she saw us, she stood up slowly and came over.

Plum said to me: 'Go and buy two pizzas. Shell likes pizza.' Then she got out of the car. I didn't hear what they said to each other but I saw they didn't embrace.

I was back within an hour, to see Shell about a hundred metres from the entrance, heading off down the road. I drove in, parked and rushed inside with the pizza boxes. Plum was slumped on the sofa in floods of tears. I'd never seen her cry like that. 'What's up?' I asked.

Plum made a violent effort to stop crying, craning her neck upwards as if she was doing the yoga salutation to the sun. Her nose was running, her face was smeared with tears and she was almost choking as she said: 'Did you see Shell?'

'Yes.'

'Go after her, quick, take her to the hotel. Then come back as fast as you can, I've got a meeting this afternoon.'

Then she slumped over and dissolved into tears again. I grabbed one of the pizzas, jumped into the car and drove along the river. There was only the one road and I reckoned Shell wouldn't have got as far as the bridge into town yet.

Shell may have been small but she walked fast and she was almost there by the time I caught up with her. I drove past and slowed down so I could keep pace with her, but she didn't stop. 'Shell, Plum wants me to take you to the hotel,' I said. She paid no attention. 'It's a fair distance,' I said. She walked on a few paces then stopped and stood stock still in the road. I was about to make another attempt to persuade her when she opened the car door and got into the passenger seat.

I got as close as I could to the Lingtsang Hotel then parked and led her across the alley and inside. When she'd checked in, I gave her the pizza: 'Plum asked me to buy it for you. She says you like pizza, right?' Shell seemed unsure of what to say, then finally forced a 'Thank you!' and took the box.

3

That afternoon, in spite of the spat with her daughter and her storm of tears, Plum fixed her make-up, put on a pair of dark glasses, and went to her meeting. Her daughter must have hurt her. I was going to hurt her too. But she'd have to get over it.

I guess everyone has their world turned upside down at some time or other, just when they least expect it. Family relationships, love affairs, work, health. Whatever it is, life's a bitch.

When I dropped Plum at Mr Ouyang's office, she said they'd be using his car to go out to dinner. She didn't need me to take her, only to pick up afterwards.

As I left, I saw the three men from the NFMIA arriving in Shao's car.

Somehow I found myself back at the Lingtsang, without really knowing what I was going to do. I saw my old mate, Norbu, the clerk at Reception, and got him to show me Shell's details. Name: Shell LIN, it said. So Shell was her real name, not just a child-hood nickname. Or if it was, they'd got so used to it, it had turned into her real, adult name. Shell, Champie – it seemed Plum liked nicknames.

I looked at the address column, but she had only written 'Beijing'.

'Hey, Norbu!' I teased him. 'That's a sloppy way of doing your job.'

'But she's your boss's guest,' he protested. 'And Plum made me give her a seventy per cent discount too!'

I asked where her room was and Norbu pointed upstairs to the first floor. 'Is she still in?' I asked.

'She hasn't stirred. Are you going up?' he said.

'No, no,' I said hastily. But I hung around anyway, maybe hoping Shell would come down. Norbu and I sat on the sofa by Reception and had a coffee and a good gossip about the girls we used to know. They were all married with kids, and some of them were divorced and on their second partner. 'That's all right, then,' I said. 'I didn't do them any harm when I dumped them.'

'And you've done OK for yourself,' said Norbu. 'Look at that car you drive and the fancy house you live in. We all look up to you, you know.'

'I thought you all called me Plum's "Tibetan Mastiff puppy"?'

'That's praise!' he said.

In the end, Shell never came out of her room. A bunch of Chinese turned up and Norbu got busy checking them in. I wandered off, crossed Beijing East Road and went down Tsomoling Alley until I got to the Shide Tratsang ruins.

This monastery had been destroyed, and for some reason never rebuilt. Now there was a big shopping mall next to it and it looked like it wouldn't be long before the monastery was handed over to the developers.

It was a pity. I had many good memories of this place. When I was at middle school, I used to bring girls to mess around here. In fact, the first time, it was a girl who brought me. My first wet kiss was here, my first grope, it all happened here. The first time for all these things felt marvellous – small steps for lips and fingers were big steps in my life. This was where my youthful longings were first satisfied, and where my youthful sexual fantasies turned into reality. Here, I had been in love and in lust. But here that confusing, but perfect, feeling of happiness had come to an end too. I grew into a man and all that was left was lust, greedy insatiable lust. I could never go back to those old feelings again.

I stayed until dusk. The rays of the setting sun lit up the traces of faded wall paintings on the ruined walls. A woman's face, maybe the Tara, or maybe not.

A thought struck me and I felt the wind blowing through those prayer flags. I hopped into the car and drove home.

I turned the sitting-room light on and had another look at the Tara statuette. I was right – it was Shell's face. Not as long and thin as hers but thinner than most Taras. Shell's expression was severe, while the Tara was serene, but there was no doubt at all this was Shell's face. True, she had Plum's mischievous twinkle, something Shell's eyes didn't have. But, whatever Plum said about the Tara looking like she had looked as a middle-school student, the resemblance was really with her daughter.

Were Shell's breasts pointy like little missiles? Or like steamed cornbreads? Suddenly, I felt fired up. But I knew I had to keep it for Plum. As long as we were together, I had to keep it all for her. But I was finding it tough.

4

When the lizard's in the water, the toads are going to jump in after it, and the lizard's only chance of survival is to swim like crazy . . . This was the gist of the conversation I overheard between Plum and Mr Ouyang.

Ouyang didn't have his driver that evening, and got into our Toyota. As soon as the car door was shut, he started effing and blinding, and Plum ranted on about shameless, bear-faced wickedness. It was obvious why Ouyang had wanted a ride with us – he and Plum had had to contain their fury at the Chinese officials while they were wining and dining them. Apparently, state-run industries were demanding a slice of the new Burma market that

Plum and Ouyang had worked so hard to develop. In fact, they wanted the lion's share. This was a sector that no one would touch up till now. But now the lizard was in the water, the toads had jumped in after it.

They cursed and swore almost all the way home, until they finally ran out of steam and agreed they'd have to just cope with it the best they could. I saw Ouyang grip Plum's hand as they sat quietly side by side. I thought that showed real concern for Plum.

After a bit, Plum took out her mobile: 'It's no good, I've got to go and have it out with Shell. I can't have her going off with everything up in the air.'

'Shell?' she said gently into the phone. 'It's Mum. Are you at the hotel? Get your things together and come home for tonight. I want to talk to you, OK? You don't need to check out, the company will settle up tomorrow. I'll be at the hotel in fifteen minutes. Wait for me there, OK?'

'That's right, you have a good talk,' said Ouyang. 'I don't understand you, what's past is past, she's your own flesh and blood, you shouldn't keep things from her.'

But Plum said: 'It's all the fault of you men.'

Ouyang puckered his lips and Plum gave him a quick kiss. I pretended I hadn't noticed.

Once we'd taken Ouyang home, we drove back into the city, and Plum gave me my instructions. 'Tomorrow, you take Shell to the airport first and then collect me. I'm flying to Kunming then taking a group to Burma for a couple of weeks.' I grunted agreement.

'I'm dead tired,' she went on. 'Just the thought of spending all that time with bigwigs from state-run businesses tires me out.'

I wanted to ask her why she and Shell had fallen out but didn't dare. I hardly ever broached personal things with Plum. 'Have you got enough cash?' she asked. 'Use the credit card if it runs out.' Plum was always very considerate like that.

Then I blurted out: 'Don't take it so hard, Plum.'

'Thank you, Champie, you're a good boy,' she said. 'You know where I've really messed up in my life? I've been a bad mother and I hurt Shell.'

'Shell—' The word slipped out of my mouth. I hastily added: 'Your daughter, she's a good girl.' But Plum wasn't paying attention.

'It's my fault she's like this. But this time, she's got completely the wrong end of the stick and I want to explain so she understands. I'm going to take a nap. Wake me when we get there.'

You can drive right up to the Lingtsang at that time of day. I got two umbrellas and waited outside the hotel. It always rains in Lhasa in the evening. Plum came out with Shell and I held one umbrella over each of them and escorted them to the car. Then I took the umbrellas back to the taxi stand. When I got back to the car, Plum was holding Shell's hand. 'Shell, that question you asked me this morning, it's been on my mind all day. You've really got the wrong end of the stick.' Shell said nothing, perhaps because I was there. 'Champa's one of the family,' Plum told her, but Shell still didn't answer. 'Fine, let's go home and talk,' Plum said finally.

When we got there, Plum told me to go and open a bottle of red wine. Plum went over to the White Tara and said: 'Shell, come and look, do you know what it is?'

'Yep.'

'What do you think?'

'It's nicely made.'

'Look at the face,' Plum pursued. 'Don't you think it looks like me?'

Shell gave her an odd look.

'That's just like me when I was at middle school.'

Shell mumbled something that might have been: 'Really? You don't say.'

I wanted to tell her: 'Shell, the Tara looks like you.'

Plum gestured to me to put the wine down in the sitting room.

They sat down and I left the room but I stayed near enough to eavesdrop.

'This is Australian – have some,' said Plum.

'Mum, I'm tired,' said Shell. 'Just say what you've got to say.'

'You said this morning you're sure you were adopted. I can't imagine where you got that idea from. Of course you're my daughter. You're completely on the wrong track if you think any different. Who told you that you were adopted?'

'Families I know where the kids are adopted are all like this,' said Shell. 'The parents won't admit it, they lie through their teeth and insist the kids are their birth children.'

'The parents only want what's best for them.'

'The kids have the right to know.'

'There are some things it's better not to know.'

'And that's why you've been lying to me all along.'

'Oh hell! How did we end up here?'

'Mum, please just tell me the truth. Don't tell me any more lies! I'm begging you. If I'm adopted, just tell me. Adopted, fostered, bought, I just want to know.'

'Of course you're my birth child, Shell. I swear I'm not lying.'

'I don't believe you.'

'Then go and ask your grandparents.'

'Whatever they say, I still won't believe them.'

'So what will make you believe me? Right, wait till I get back to Beijing and I'll go home and get you your birth certificate.'

'Even the birth certificate wouldn't make me believe you. You're quite capable of waving your magic wand and conjuring up anything you want, *dzi* beads, sacred relics, *shahtoosh* wool . . . '

'What have they got to do with anything? What are you getting at?'

'Didn't you fix me a school-leaving certificate? Is there anything you can't fix?'

'That's not a fake, it was a real certificate.'

'The certificate's real, I know, but the marks on it are made up.'

'Shell, you're being so unfair. Tell me, what would make you believe I'm your real mum?'

'Telling me who my father is! I don't care what happened, I'm OK with anything, I just want to know. Then I can stop torment-ing myself. It's as simple as that. Mum, please take pity on me and tell me who my dad is. And where he is.'

'And that's what all this is about? You just want me to tell you who your dad is, right?'

'You've got a boyfriend now, can't you forgive my dad?'

'Shell, it's not like that!'

'I don't care how many boyfriends you've got, that's nothing to do with me. You're my mum and you've been my mum all my life. But the family has no right to keep from me who my dad is.'

'And that bastard's now got a daughter who's protecting him!'

'I'm not protecting him. All my life your family's called him a bastard, I don't have any problem with that. I think he's a bastard too. But I want to know that bastard's name. Give me a photo so I can see what kind of a bastard he is. If he's dead, then I can go and find the death certificate. You can't carry on, year after year, not telling me. You said he was a bastard to abandon me when I was just a few months old, so why won't you say any more? Even if he's a murderer, a philanderer, a rapist, a traitor, or seduced you, or raped you, I wouldn't give a toss. I can take it, however bad it is!'

'You're right. I know this is my problem, it's just something I can't get past.'

'What did he do that you can't tell me?'

'Give me a bit of time.'

'What did he do that you can't tell me?'

'I can't tell you right now. Give me a bit of time.'

'So I'm adopted.'

'Shell, don't start that again.'

'I'm adopted. I'm adopted. I'm adopted!'

'Shell, please! Don't be like that!'

'I'm going to bed. Wake me up when you've made up your mind to tell me.'

Shell went into the bedroom and shut the door. Plum slumped back on the sofa and burst into tears again. But then she made a big effort to stop and, face streaming with tears, went into the bedroom too.

There was no sound from the bedroom. I stayed in the sitting room, thinking I'd sleep in the guest room that night. I drank most of the bottle. Then Plum came back in and sat down on the sofa. 'Put your arms around me, Champie,' she said. I did, and then started to rub myself against her, but she said: 'No, not tonight. I'm tired and I'm sad and I hurt too much. Champie, I'll be away for eleven days.' Then she grabbed me and I said: 'Let's do a "spurt of the moment".' This time she didn't say no. I thought of the Tara, then of Shell. Shell, Tara, Tara, Shell. The Tara merged into Shell and I wasn't thinking of the Tara any more, only of Shell. Plum stopped my mouth with her hand and I realized she hadn't been making her usual noises. I finished silently, and she came off without a sound either.

5

That night, I thought of Shell. The next day, Shell avoided my eyes. In fact, she looked sterner than ever. But my heart was going pitter-patter like when I was a youngster, a youngster sneaking off with a girl to the Shide Tratsang ruins.

This youngster was besotted with a girl who hadn't a clue how he felt.

She didn't meet my eyes once in the car either. She probably despised me, even found me disgusting.

To her, I was just her mum's Tibetan mastiff puppy.

To me, she was my Tara, my life, and she was the only one who could save me now.

It was pointless wondering whether this was love or lust. I didn't know. Just the same as when I was a young guy chasing girls – I didn't see the difference then either. I only knew that she, Shell, was the one for me. I wanted her, I wanted to sleep with her in my arms, cheek to cheek, adoring her, smelling her, biting her, fucking her, murmuring 'Shell! Shell!' into her ear.

I was in love, and that was that. I'd leave Plum like a man, because I was in love with another woman, who just happened to be Plum's daughter. I'd give up the life all my mates envied, for love, and no one could say anything about that.

But how was I going to tell her? Shell had absolutely no idea how much I loved and needed her, absolutely no idea I couldn't live without her. I was stymied. She was about to leave and she loathed and despised me. If she left like that, that was the end of us. I'd never get another chance. I'd fall back into hell and there would be no one to rescue me.

'Was the pizza nice?' I said, thinking of her hesitation when I gave her the pizza yesterday.

It seemed to take her a while to realize I was talking to her.

'That pizza I bought you yesterday, you like pizzas, right?'

She corrected me sullenly: 'No, I don't like pizza at all.'

'But your mum said you did.'

'She remembered wrong, I haven't liked pizza for ages. My mum doesn't have any idea what food I like.'

I was just about to say something else when she went on: 'I don't want to talk about my mum.'

'But your mum—' I said.

She turned and glared me. 'I don't want to talk about my mum, OK?'

'Me and your mum—' I said.

'Please – don't – mention – my – mum!'

She didn't want to talk about her mum with me, she despised me. I couldn't help blurting out: 'I'm not your mum's dog!'

She stared at me for a moment, then snapped: 'Don't you give dogs a bad name!' Then she turned back and sat staring forwards.

We arrived at the airport and she got out without a word. I'd lost any chance of changing her opinion of me.

I leaned over the passenger seat and shouted out of the car window at her: 'Shell, it's you the Tara looks like!' And then I drove off without waiting to see if she'd heard me or not.

An hour or so later, I got a text from Shell: 'Champa, I was wrong to behave like that. I'm sorry. I'm on board the plane now. Thank you for looking after me. Shell'

6

Shell and Plum had both gone. I'd taken Shao and the clients from the NFMIA to the airport too. She'd gone, the little guy was still excited, and the big guy felt like he was stuck fast in a pot of glue. I'd stay at home, in bed. That way, we'd see what the little guy wanted and the big guy could get a move on too. I had a lot of thinking to do.

But Lhasa was small and news travelled fast. With Plum gone, some old schoolmates wanted to catch up with me and I tried to put them off but Norbu said that they'd been putting it off for days because of me, the whole point of the get-together was that Tsering was here, and if we waited any longer he'd be gone.

Tsering was an engineer at the meteorological office. He graduated from the Meteorology Institute in Nanjing and was assigned a government job in a Khamdo village – this was the policy now, everyone assigned to a government bureau in Lhasa had to do a stint in the villages. It was no joke being sent to work among these poor nomadic communities, especially for us city boys. Tsering's bosses were pretty decent to their staff, and allowed them a few days' leave in Lhasa every six months, which they took in turn. At the Tibetan New Year, Tsering hadn't made it back, so here he was now.

That evening, we went for a meal at the Phin Tsok Ge Don in Tuanjie New Village. The others were all college graduates, and we always used to talk about jobs, getting a house, where we'd been on holiday and so on, when we met up. But this time, everyone was full of gripes.

We asked Tsering what he did in his village office. He said every day he had to read the Tibetan newspapers aloud to the herders, even though they couldn't understand a word because of his Lhasa accent. 'Don't ask me anything else!' he went on. 'I got sent there and that's that. I don't even know if I can get back after I've done my year. We've been told that these stints might be extended to three years.'

Tashi had his gripes too, even though he had a cushy job in the government. He'd started as a primary school teacher and then got the transfer he'd been hankering after, and was running a Lhasa monastery. The local government was starting to run training courses for monastery administrators and primary teachers were being fast-tracked because they were better educated. The transfer automatically made him a government officer, and gave him status and much better treatment than a teacher got. We congratulated him on his lucky break, but he said the monastery was a nest of vipers, everyone was at each other's throats. It was really hard work and it was getting him down. He wife sat beside him not saying a word, but she must have been pretty happy. After all, Tashi was living and working in Lhasa now.

Even Tenzin was out of sorts today. That made me mad. Out of all of us, he was the only one to graduate from the University of Tibet and go on to get a job in the police. Of all of us, he had the brightest prospects. He taught at the police college, and big changes were afoot there. The Chinese government was pouring money into the 'Stability Preservation' campaign and there was a drive to recruit Tibetans to the police. But today Tenzin was whingeing about his increased workload and saying he was exhausted. Plus, he said, soldiers got better benefits than the police. His brother had graduated from a university in China but had still never managed to get posted to Lhasa . . . on and on he went.

What I was thinking was, you're all on the Stability Preservation Campaign bandwagon and the future's rosy. However hard the work is, at least you're going places. What about me, what am I supposed to do? I had no one to talk to about it and it was all getting me down.

When Tenzin went to the bathroom, Norbu told us that Tenzin's gran had been to India and was made to study her 'errors' when she came back. The experience put her in hospital, and it seemed she wasn't going to pull through. Tenzin hadn't said anything about that to us.

After dinner, Tsering, Tenzin and Tashi and his wife wanted to play *mahjong*, and Norbu and I left, saying we were going to play billiards. We were the only two who hadn't been to university or college.

Norbu said he wanted to go to Gama Gunsang to see his mum, and I drove him there. I felt like a drive, it would clear my head.

In the car, Norbu told me that his hotel's main investor had decided to ditch the local tour companies and link up with the high-end Chinese tourism network. There were new restrictions on foreigners touring in Tibet and you couldn't rely on them as a source of business. In any case, visitors from China were bigger spenders.

He reckoned that I was better off than him and had nothing to get depressed about. But what the hell did he know about the mess I was in? They all had a profession, I was just someone's Tibetan mastiff puppy.

Gama Gunsang was the district of Lhasa I liked best. An aunt of mine and her family bought a plot here in the 1980s, and built themselves a house. As a kid, I often used to go and play there. My aunt and Norbu's mum were neighbours and were in the same local residents' community group. They spent all their time planning outings, and dinners, and picnics and so on. Often I used to go along too. Then my aunt's employers gave her a new flat in the northern outskirts of Lhasa, and they sold the house.

My aunt always regretted that. She still missed Gama Gunsang.

It was a few years since I'd taken the car there, especially at night, because the road was terrible. The government kept promising to fix the potholes but nothing happened. Maybe they were going to let the road go completely and then flatten the whole area. Gama Gunsang was known as Lhasa's Saddam City – it had the largest concentration of Tibetan residents of all the districts of Lhasa city.

I knew the road to Norbu's home like the back of my hand, which was a good thing as there were no signposts or street lights. We jolted over the potholes in the dark, with me trusting to my instincts. I realized that Gama Gunsang was still a part of me.

7

The next morning, I went to the shop. Only A-Lan and Jigme were there. A-Lan was in a relaxed mood so I took my chance and got her talking about Shell.

She said Shell had always been a thorn in her mum's side. There were endless problems and rows. I coaxed her into saying more. Plum was originally from Nanjing, and had graduated from Nanjing Normal University. Shell was born there. When Plum wanted to go and work in Beijing, she left Shell with her mum. It worked OK when she was a little girl, but when Shell started middle school, the grandparents began to feel she was too much of a handful. They were getting on in years, they wanted to enjoy life, and they didn't have the energy to keep a rebellious teenager under control. It all came to a head one night during the summer holidays, when Shell didn't come home. She said she'd gone to the house of a boy in her class and they'd stayed up all night playing World of Warcraft. Meantime, the grandparents sat up waiting for her, worried out of their minds. For a girl just starting middle school to stay out all night with a boy was a big deal for the old couple, but Shell wouldn't admit she'd done anything wrong. In fact, she was aggrieved that they didn't trust her.

For years, I used to play World of Warcraft. In fact, it got so I wasn't sleeping or eating properly and was skiving off work. There were a few girls who stayed up with us, out of loyalty, but they just sat and watched.

Anyway, after that night, Shell's grandparents gave up on her and told Plum to come and take her back. Plum was putting every ounce of energy into her job and had no time to look after a rebellious daughter, so she sent her to a boarding school on the outskirts of Beijing, A-Lan wasn't sure which, apparently one with a high pass rate for university entrance exams. But Shell was always bunking off class and getting into trouble. She ran away a few times and then dropped out. She wouldn't have got a school-leaving certificate at all if Plum hadn't been friends with the head and begged a favour.

'Real certificate, fake marks,' I commented.

'Exactly,' said A-Lan. 'Whenever Plum talks about that time with Shell, she bursts into floods of tears. That girl really gave her a hard time.'

'I saw Plum in floods of tears, just yesterday,' I said. 'Shell really upset her. I can't understand what Shell blames her mother for.'

'Right. They've never got on, though. You've seen they're not close, always at loggerheads.'

'What about Shell's dad?' I asked.

'A bastard. According to Plum, he abandoned them when Shell was a few months old. One of those. But that was in Nanjing, before I knew Plum. I don't know much about him, and Plum doesn't like to talk about that period of her life,' said A-Lan. Then she went on: 'See the friends I've got now? They're all from my middle school, and some of them even from my primary school. We keep in touch online, and every time I go to Beijing, we meet up. But I've never seen Plum with her school or college friends, not once. I've known her since she arrived in Beijing. That was twenty years ago, and I know that all the friends she has now are from after she arrived there. She won't talk about her Nanjing days even to me, except maybe to say that she was a bit of a glamour girl at university, had a fantastic social life and got good marks too. According to her, she and that worthless SOB of a husband were such brilliant students that she never understood how they'd had a daughter like Shell. I don't know why she and Shell's father split up, she's never said. Later on, she brought her parents to Beijing to live, and I did meet them. They're educated people and were banged up in a May 7 Cadre School during the Cultural Revolution. That was where Plum was conceived. They were both getting on a bit, but Plum's mother had her baby and kept her.'

I interrupted: 'Is it possible that Shell was adopted and Plum isn't her birth mother? Maybe that's why she turned out so different from her mum and never took to her school work?'

'You mean that Plum and her husband couldn't have children, so they adopted Shell, and then the husband left?'

'Something like that, yes.'

'What an idiotic thing to say! Plum was only twenty-two or twenty-three then, and they hadn't been married long, why would they adopt?'

'Maybe Plum adopted as a single parent and there never was a husband.'

'That's even more unlikely. You didn't choose to be a single mother in those days. Besides, Plum was such a stunner, she must have had men after her in droves. Why would she have bothered to adopt?'

'Maybe she was someone's mistress,' I ventured.

'Now you're being really daft! Who d'you take her for? Besides, she's a tough one, you know that. The wife wouldn't have stood a chance if Plum wanted her husband. I did wonder once whether Shell was illegitimate . . . maybe Plum had an affair with an important official or something so they had to keep the child secret.

But then I thought that couldn't be true either, because Plum's had to work so hard all her life. If the father was a bigwig, he'd have given her a helping hand for sure and she would never have had all this trouble.'

A-Lan had lost me there. But, in any case, I was still pursuing my own train of thought and wasn't going to be side-tracked. 'Could Plum have been raped and got pregnant, do you think?'

'Don't be stupid. Even if she'd left it too late for an abortion, she needn't have given Shell the father's surname like she did. I thought about that too.'

'So then why doesn't Plum want to tell Shell who her father is?'

A-Lan went all deep on me. 'Everyone has secrets, don't they? Champa, there are some things you should steer clear of. You seem to be getting on really well with Plum, so don't spoil it.'

I decided to change the subject. 'Can I ask you something, A-Lan? What does "give a dog a bad name" mean?'

'Give a dog a bad name,' said A-Lan, 'means the person you're talking about behaves worse than a dog, so calling them a dog is insulting to dogs.'

Why had Shell said that to me? It was so hurtful.

But then I remembered that she had apologized in her text to me. And she'd finished it: 'Thanks for looking after me, Shell'. Oh, Shell, what were you up to? Saying such vile things and then saying sorry, and thanking me. I felt a jolt of lightning and suddenly I was on fire. I had to go and find her! I told A-Lan I was going to see my gran in Shigatse and asked her to phone me if anything came up. I asked her to do me a favour and go and water Plum's plants every other day. She'd do what I asked, I knew how to sweet-talk a woman.

I withdrew twenty Mao-notes from the ATM – 2,000 *yuan* – went home, and gave the car a quick wash. I got my phone charger, iPad and GPS, and stuffed a big backpack with a change of clothes. Then I chucked hard biscuits, a big bag of black sesame paste, instant noodles and mineral water into a box, as I always did for a long journey, and added four bottles of red wine. Finally, I wrapped the Tara figurine in a silk *khata*, put it in a small bag and threw everything into the Range Rover.

I had a bit more than nine days. Four to get there, four to get back and a day or so in Beijing to talk to Shell. Of course, I might never find her or she might refuse to see me and yell at me and then kick me out, or phone her mum and say I'd betrayed her. Or then again, after my trip to Beijing, I might never come back to Lhasa again.

Chapter Three

1

THAT DAY, I must have taken thousands of lives in the space of less than twenty minutes. Along the highway, I drove smack into the middle of a midge storm.

It felt like they were launching a concerted attack, spattering against my windscreen like flurries of rain. Every few seconds the wipers cleared a pulp of their little corpses away and I'd be able to see out but in no time at all the glass was blurry again.

All these crash victims were looking for mates, I knew that. They'd reached that crazy time in their lives when males and females emerged and threw themselves into the mating dance, until finally they paired off. It was a cloudy day and the bright beams of passing cars' headlights were a deadly lure. They danced out into the open from the darkness of the undergrowth and the trees, possessed by the frenzied urge for sex, instinct making them reckless of the danger. And they offered themselves up, unresisting, as sacrificial victims to humans and machinery. It was pointless carnage, but at least enough survived to get on with mating and ensuring the continuance of the family line.

Not that this was going to stop any of the cars. We humans had no choice in the matter. We just had to keep ploughing on so we could get through the besieging swarm. Some drivers actually put their foot down for the thrill of ramming the insects as hard and as fast as possible.

In the past, I used to speed up too. I had fantasies of being a hero on the field of battle, clad in a tiger-skin cloak and turquoise-studded armour, wielding a broadsword, charging the enemy formations on my steed, slashing off heads as if they were melons, chopping victims' flesh as if it were meat, invincible, as my 4x4 slammed into swarms of midges.

But today I didn't. I was wondering why we'd come across the midge storm just here. They were usually confined to the Tuotuo River and Naij Tal in Qinghai, but now here they were on the Changtang plateau, and in greater numbers than I'd ever seen them. It had been sixteen or seventeen degrees the last few days, and that must have made them pupate. It just so happened that today was windless and overcast and we were all driving with our headlights on, and I had set out late from Lhasa. It was pure chance that, at section fifteen of the highway, I hit the midge storm. A bit earlier or a bit later, and I could have avoided this replay of *Cars and Guns 3D*. But the midges' fate and mine had collided and I was going to be the instrument of their destruction. They couldn't avoid it and neither could I.

Even if they didn't die now, their lives would be over within a couple of days of mating. Still, they'd have tasted the sweetness of sex, completed their life cycle and died a natural death. But who decided which ones got to survive and enjoy the sweetness of sex and which ones died prematurely, which thousand expired on my windscreen and which two thousand on the windscreen of the approaching truck? It was probably completely random. If so, how could I avoid killing them? Did I have a choice in the matter? All drivers left roadkill behind them. If you got trapped in the midge storm, you couldn't avoid committing murder. We all had blood on our hands, we were all guilty. I had lost the pleasure I used to get from hitting the midges, but I couldn't stop killing and killing and killing.

Their corpses gathered in layers at the bottom of the windscreen and collected in the corners the wipers couldn't reach. And
those were the bits I could see. It was too bad I'd just washed
my white Range Rover. Midges were dirty creatures; they carried
disease and bit people. (There was a good reason they were called
'nippers'.) Some of them were blood-suckers too.

Die then! The quicker you die, the quicker you'll be reincarnated.

2

I calculated that I needed to get to Tanggula checkpoint by the
end of the first day. That was 700 kilometres from Lhasa, and the
middle section had speed restrictions. I hadn't foreseen the midge
storm but, in any case, it hadn't slowed me down.

Strange to think that, when I got up this morning, I had no idea
I'd be on my way to Beijing. It was talking to A-Lan that gave me
this overwhelming urge for a road trip . . . the urge to have one
final fling and throw myself into the mating dance with Shell.

I sat by the stove in a Hui Muslim guesthouse near the Tanggula
Hot Springs military camp. I ate their mutton, drank my red wine,
and felt no desire to talk to anyone. Nearby, three other Tibetans
were sitting over their dinner. Two had on army uniforms so were
probably young soldiers from the army camp, the other perhaps
their friend or relative, or a teacher – he talked alternately in
Chinese and Tibetan. His Tibetan was the standard Lhasa variety,
peppered with the kind of dialect expressions the other two used.
The three of them were discussing some black bears which had
been seen near the army post.

'I tell you, I saw them with my own eyes,' said one soldier.
'Eight of them.'

'They scavenge for food leftovers from the army camp,' the
older one said. 'It's good stuff.'

'You're right,' said the younger one. 'They've developed a taste
for it, even numbing-hot Sichuan pepper.'

'It's a shame,' complained the teacher, 'all the food that gets chucked out.'

'You're right,' said the older soldier, 'but it can't be helped. More people means more leftovers. The food budget goes up every year so of course they've got to throw the surplus out. If they cut down, next year's budget would be cut, and so would their rake-off.'

'Right!' agreed the teacher. 'Whatever you do, stuff will get thrown out, even if we eat as much as we can.'

The older soldier laughed. 'No chance of eating it all. Half gets siphoned off, then we eat a quarter and throw away the rest.'

The younger soldier put in: 'You just go to the river and you'll see how much food is thrown away every day.'

'It doesn't matter,' said the older one. 'If humans don't eat it, the beasts will.'

'Hey,' said the young soldier, 'our bears are the best fed in the world! They get big portions of fish and meat for dinner every day!'

'Right!' said the teacher. 'This place attracts bears from all over Tibet and Kokonor. After they've fed here, they don't know how to hunt for themselves any more.'

'Well, that doesn't matter,' said the older of the soldiers. 'While there are troops stationed here, the bears don't need to worry that food rations will dry up.'

'So long as there's the army camp, the bears'll have no problem!' agreed the younger one.

'Right, right, the chickens can dance on the roof all they like but it'll never cave in,' said the teacher. 'The army camp will always be here. So they can keep the bears fed, can't they?'

The waiter came over to me and said in a low voice: 'Tonight, uh, want me to take you to see the bears at the river? You drive, eh?'

'Are you crazy?' I said. 'I need my sleep.'

Plum called at night and I went outside to talk, and told her I was in Shigatse, seeing my gran. The dogs were barking like crazy – maybe there really were bears around.

Early next morning, as soon as the petrol station was open, I went to fill up and gave the car a wash. Someone was there before me, a middle-aged man who looked like a local, in a shabby old Xiali which might have been a taxi in a former life. I'd driven a Xiali once. Like all small, China-produced cars, it was very economical on the petrol. I felt quite nostalgic.

The teacher from last night's dinner hurried into the petrol station. He looked at the Xiali, no doubt thinking it was too dirty, then walked over to me. I knew he was going to ask for a lift. He addressed me in standard Tibetan: 'Good morning! Are you going to Golmud?' I nodded but didn't say anything. We watched the Xiali with the local man inside drive off.

The teacher waited patiently while I cleared the corpses of the midges from the windscreen, then got in the car with me. 'My name's Nyima,' he said.

'Champa,' I introduced myself. I had almost said 'Champie'. I glowered to discourage any further conversation. He could count his lucky stars he had a lift in a new Range Rover Aurora 4x4 instead of a dirty old Xiali.

3

It was a bizarre crash. And we were first on the scene.

We had passed Yanshiping and were heading towards Golmud. I knew the road well and put my foot down. It was a sunny day, visibility was good and so was the road surface. In the distance, we could see shy Tibetan antelope, but still I didn't say anything and Nyima was quiet too. It wasn't going to be a chatty journey.

It appeared in the distance after we'd been going an hour. As we got closer, I saw it was the old Xiali which had collided with a 4x4. It must have just happened, but we didn't see or hear anything. I pulled in and before we'd stopped, Nyima was out of the car and running over.

The oncoming vehicle was a Volvo XC90. The female passenger was clutching a mobile phone and trying to extricate herself from the air bag. Nyima and I hauled her out of the car and carried her to the roadside. 'I can't see out of one eye,' she muttered. I guessed the impact might have detached her retina, but I didn't say so.

I went around the back of the Volvo to the driver's side. The man still had his seat belt on and was not moving. Half his face was plastered in blood and goo, and fragments of broken glass were stuck to it. He'd had it, I thought. But air was leaking from the inflated air bag, so it must have functioned at the moment of impact. The steering wheel was slightly wonky but the instrument panel was only dented, not badly damaged. Surely the driver's head couldn't have hit the windscreen but, if not, where had all the blood come from? That kind of windscreen was shatterproof even when it cracked. What had hit the man? I glanced sideways at him. Though his face was covered in blood, behind his sunglasses, his eyes were not bloodshot. He blinked. He was alive, and conscious. Maybe he was in shock, or he might have hit his head on the steering wheel. 'He's alive,' I said to Nyima, on the other side of the car.

I moved over to the Xiali, dreading what I was going to see. The front of the car had almost disappeared: the bonnet, the radiator screen, the wings and the headlights had been crushed flat as a pancake. That is, the whole engine was stoved in. The driver, the middle-aged man we had seen that morning, was mashed to a bloody pulp, so entangled with the car parts you could hardly see where his limbs began and ended. I couldn't make out if he had a seat belt on or not but in this kind of crash it wouldn't have made any difference. As the front of the car was pushed inside, a sharp edge must have hit his neck and sliced his head off so it shot through the shattered windscreen. It was his head which had

made the tennis-ball-sized hole in the Volvo windscreen. I turned
to look. It was only then that I saw the head was still stuck there.
That was where the blood on the Volvo driver's head had come
from.

Nyima came and stood on the Volvo's dented bumper, and
leaned over to whisper something in the ear of the decapitated
head.

I went to the driver's side, gently removed the man's sunglasses
and put them in his coat pocket. 'You're all right,' I said to him.

The woman we'd moved earlier to the roadside shouted:
'Mister, mister, where are we? *Tashi delek! Ni hao!* Do you speak
Mandarin?'

I took the mobile from her and spoke into it. 'We're at
Yanshiping, heading for Golmud, a bit before section nine. Our
position is 109-3135 or 3136 or thereabouts. Yes . . . one dead,
two injured . . . right!'

I gave the woman back her phone. 'Twenty minutes, they said.'
She thanked me.

'Have you got an overcoat in your suitcase?' I asked the woman.
She squinted suspiciously at me, one eye tight shut. I opened the
case and found two thick coats. I gave one to her and took the
other to the man and put it around him. 'The ambulance will
be here in twenty minutes,' I told him. 'Better keep still for the
moment.' The man blinked. Nyima, meanwhile, was still talking
to the decapitated head.

It struck me then that it was such a clear day and visibility was
so good, these two vehicles really shouldn't have collided.

Probably both cars had crossed into the oncoming lane, and
the drivers had tried to turn back into their own lane just before
impact. So they'd met head on, and the blood and brains of the
Xiali driver's head had spattered all over the face of the Volvo
driver.

I figured it had happened like this: the Xiali driver had been
driving fast, probably because he knew the road pretty well,

which was why I hadn't caught him up in the Range Rover. The Chinese couple had their trip well planned and were on the road from Golmud about four or five in the morning. That was how they'd got this far. They both had their seat belts done up and were in a Volvo 4x4, the ultimately safe car if you were going to prang someone or be pranged because it had a special collision mitigating system. The point of impact was at the same level as for other cars, but that was fair enough, you couldn't have big cars bearing down on the smaller ones. Of course, in a real high-speed collision, the damage caused depended on the strength of the chassis and other safety design features. The oddest thing was that all three people must have been asleep, even if it was only for a second or two. There was no other explanation. Otherwise, they would not have collided on the open road. So – both drivers dropped off and veered into the oncoming lane. They woke up at the last moment and instinctively swerved back into their own lanes and collided head on. If one had made the best of a bad job and turned into the oncoming lane instead, the crash might not have been so deadly. Life really was a bitch, there was no other way of putting it. As it was, the two who were in the newer car, with the highest safety spec, may have got the fright of their lives but they only suffered high-impact injuries, while the man driving the shabby little Xiali was pulped and decapitated. The odds really had been stacked against him.

Nyima came over to me. 'We're just about finished here, aren't we?'

I agreed. We couldn't waste any more time, we should be on our way. Nyima seemed even keener to get away than me. Just at that moment, a party of five pilgrims passed by, prostrating themselves all the way, pushing a motorbike with a two-wheeled cart attached behind it. Help would be along soon, and the Chinese couple would be fine. So we drove off.

4

I began to talk to Nyima. 'Are you a monk?' I asked.

'Not really,' he said, vaguely.

'But weren't you reciting the *Bardo* prayer for the dead?'

'Not really . . . '

'So what were you whispering to that . . . that head, that took you so long?'

'I was telling him to be sure to remember his lama teacher and everything his lama teacher said to him.'

'Could he hear you?'

'I don't know. I just talked as if he could hear, I hope he could. You know someone's consciousness is supposed to survive after the body dies. When it's a sudden death, maybe the soul hangs around the scene for a bit.'

'But why did you need to get so close to him and whisper right into his ear?' I asked.

'Eh? Right! Of course I didn't need to. If he was going to hear, he'd hear anyway. I just thought he'd hear a bit clearer if I got close.' And he smiled self-consciously.

'Are you a teacher?' I asked.

'Not really.' He was still being vague.

'So what do you do?' I persisted.

'Hmm, how shall I put this? I don't do anything. Really. I hate that question. As soon as I say I don't do anything, I feel like I'm lying and no one'll believe me.'

'You don't do anything? Have you always done nothing?'

'How shall I put this? OK. I'm not going to lie to you, it's only been the last few years that I've done nothing, since 2008 to be precise. 2008, you remember, right? It was after that, I started to do nothing.'

I remembered all right. My aunt always said that after 2008, Lhasa was never the same again. I also remembered that I had no money coming in for months in 2008, and Plum took me on as her driver when she came back to Lhasa in the summer.

'What do you do?' Nyima asked me.

'Driving,' I said briefly, thinking I wasn't going to lie to him either but I also didn't want him to ask me any more about it. 'Do you drive?' I asked him.

He flapped his hands. 'Oh, no, I wouldn't dare. I've got a death wish.'

'A what wish?'

'A death wish. Like, if I stand on the edge of a cliff, I'm terrified I might jump. And on a railway platform, I don't dare stand too near the edge in case when the train comes in I might be overcome with the urge to jump in front of it. If I drove a car, I'd be scared I might randomly drive into a tree. Do you have that kind of a death wish?'

'You're crazy!' I said. 'Oh, sorry, I didn't mean that. No, no, I don't have a death wish.'

'Do you get sex urges?'

'Are you joking? Of course I do. Every day. Only for women, mind.'

'Some people say that we've all got both the sex urge and the death wish. Sexual desire, the desire for death, eros, thanatos, the life principle and the death principle, they go by all those names.'

'I've only got the sex urge, plus sexual desire and eros, or whatever it is.'

'Have you ever wanted to kill yourself?' he asked.

'Are you crazy?'

'Into S and M?'

'That's weird.'

'Have you ever been violent, aggressive, destructive, or reckless, or hated, punished, dominated or tortured anyone? Did you set ants on fire when you were a kid, or break girls' toys? Have you ever done extreme sports or driven fast cars?'

'Are you talking about a sex urge or . . .'

'. . . a death wish,' he finished.

'Are there only those two?' I asked.

'Some people say there are only those two and various combinations of them. Freud said that Nirvana is a kind of death wish but I don't believe that. I think that the search for Nirvana is a different kind of human desire, though it's still a desire. The way I see it, we have three kinds of desire, for sex, for death and for Nirvana.'

'Nirvana? You mean Buddhist Nirvana?' I asked incredulously.

'Right, right. You're asking me if it's distinct from the sex urge and the death wish? Well, Nirvana is stillness, emptiness, idleness, inaction, being calm, saving one's energy, minimalism. Really being free and at ease with oneself, *tathagata*, that's all part of it. Why are people always in search of peace? Because of this desire for Nirvana. The desire to live without thinking, without worldly temptations, without having to be involved in society, to just do nothing at all.'

I thought he was getting a bit too mystical. 'Isn't it hard, doing nothing?'

'It certainly is hard to do absolutely nothing. You've got to remember that there's still the sex urge and the death wish working away in us. Then there's greed and ignorance driving us to keep doing this and that all day too. The sex urge and the death wish are always working away inside us, aren't they? But the desire for Nirvana is both inactive and non-negative, non-dual and complete emptiness. What I mean is, it's very important to understand how to do nothing, and to do nothing if there's no need to do anything. Once you start doing things, there's so much to do, things get chaotic and it becomes impossible to achieve boundlessness. I once saw an old Italian film called *The Decameron*, hardly anyone saw it in China, and in it there was a sentence which went something like this: "Dreams are so good, why do we need to make them reality?" Where there are expectations, there's always disappointment. Don't expect anything. No good ever comes from expectation. Every human life depends on a breath, right? But we always forget that, except when we're gasping on our deathbeds, when we're seriously ill or in pain or have altitude sickness. Or we're having sex and we can't get it up, or we've got urine retention or constipation, or we regulate our breath and meditate or do prostrations and achieve a state of Great Perfection. At that point, we might get the feeling that every human life depends on a breath. Prisoners sometimes get that feeling too, and so do I, when I take a crap. Trouble is, I forget it when the crap's over. I'm guessing that long-distance drivers like you, driving on your own, do too. We're all born naked and every human life depends on a breath.'

I was getting fed up with all this babbling. 'Are you really not a monk or a teacher?' I asked.

'Nope.'

'What do you live on then, if you don't do anything?'

'Well, sometimes friends . . . they invite me over for a chat and give me dinner and a bed for the night. Most of the time I just leave it to fate, like today I met you and got a ride in a nice car.'

'You nearly got into the Xiali,' I pointed out.

'Right.'

'The luck of the draw.'

'Right.'

'If you'd got in the Xiali,' I said, 'it would have been a case of "blood's sicker than water".'

'Blood's sicker than water?' He laughed. 'That's an interesting way of putting it, you're absolutely right. It really would have been blood's sicker than water.'

'Are you going to Golmud to see a friend?' I asked.

'Actually, no. I'm off to . . . to Xining. Are you going through Xining?'

'Didn't you say you were going to Golmud this morning?'

'I'm really going to Xining but I thought you wouldn't want to take me that far, so I said Golmud because it was nearer.'

It occurred to me I'd have to spend the night with this guy if I took him to Xining.

He seemed to sense what I was thinking. 'It doesn't matter,' he said, 'you just let me out at Golmud, right?'

'Tell me more about the sex urge thing,' I said, still puzzled.

'The sex urge . . . hmmm . . . that'll take quite a long time,' he said.

I bought him lunch at Golmud. We argued over who should pay but I politely insisted and he gave in. We thought we'd eat mutton but we were put off by the smell of the broth and decided to go vegetarian. We found somewhere that did Shaanxi food and had a big bowl of plain noodles and two steamed buns. After lunch, we got to Lake Kokonor and Nyima persuaded me to go off the highway and stop in the Tibetan town of Black Horse River. In the local guesthouse, we got a three-bed room for 15 *yuan* each including hot showers. Lhasa to Beijing was nearly 4,000 kilometres and I only had 2,176 kilometres to go now.

5

As he ate, Nyima chattered continuously. It could have been irritating, but he was such a good talker that it made you want to go on listening all the same.

Some of it was a lot of rubbish, like death was the transformation of organic to inorganic. It made me think of a tourist from Hong Kong who was always saying: 'Mum's a woman.' Well, of course, that was obvious. Nyima said that when you dreamed, you were neither alert nor confused, and dreams were neither intentional nor unintentional, neither reality nor unreality. He talked like a lama, in couplets. Something was neither this nor that . . . it made my head spin.

He got very profound when it came to sex, and came out with stuff like 'sex is the essence of life', 'sex is energy', 'the body is sacred', 'the body is the last bit of the revolution's capital', 'without the body we have nothing' and more mystic twaddle, on and on.

Nyima probably didn't realize it, but the way he went on about oral fixation, anal fixation and genital fixation scared me. I had a genital fixation but I reckoned he had oral and anal fixations, the way he talked about crapping all the time. I reckoned he can't have had much sexual experience because everything he said came out of a book, and he was always quoting other people, whether it was Tantric masters or Chinese sages or foreign scholars. Just for a joke, I stuck my tongue out reverentially at him and started to address him as 'Guru Nyima' and 'Khenpo Nyima' – and he thought I was serious.

I took in more of what he was saying when he said that love and relationships between men and women and so on were a product of the sex instinct. I felt that my longing to have sex with the Tara was just because I was under too much sexual stress and this had turned into love for the Tara, and the goddess wouldn't blame me for it.

But was it my sex urge that was driving my decision to go to Beijing? Did I really want to get off with Shell so badly? Or was it just an excuse to break it off with Plum? Not 'intentional', but not 'non-intentional' either. My sex urge must be well and truly repressed. The thought made me smile.

We were passing through Dulan, an area infested with rabbits. Corpses lay littered along the roadside, some still fresh and bloody, others flattened and sun-dried. It seemed Nyima preferred death to sex. Dirty jokes were my thing, but he was full of stories about violence and death.

Take torture . . . he told me there was an ancient Tibetan way of gouging out eyes. They didn't simply gouge them out of their sockets, they got two yak knee bones, fastened them together with a leather belt and pressed a bone against each temple. Then, using a stick, they twisted the belt tighter and tighter until the eyeballs popped out, after which the sockets would be filled with boiling oil. Lungshar Dorje Tsegyal, the leader of the reform faction in the Kashag governing council, suffered this form of torture in 1934. At the time, the torturer only succeeded in squeezing out one eyeball, and had to cut the other out with a knife before filling both sockets with the oil. 'What a time the 1930s were, eh?' Nyima said, imperturbably. 'Fancy inflicting such cruel punishment on the reformers. Right up until the end of the 1940s, there was constant in-fighting between the regent lama, the Sera monastery and the Tibetan nobility. It was so stupid. The situation must have looked hopeless so it's no wonder young Lhasa idealists like Baba Phuntsok Wangyal wanted to go over to the Communist Party. The authorities back then were simply blind to what was happening around them.'

I found two girls, both called Dromazo, and brought them back to our room to give us a foot massage. Nyima turned out to have a low pain threshold and made an incredible fuss. 'A-ya! Buddha, Dharma, Sangha! A-ya! I must be a masochist to do this! A-ya! My eyes are going to pop out of my head! Goddess that Devours Ten Thousand Tents,' he shrieked, 'I love you to bits!' He made such a noise that when Plum phoned, I had to go outside to take the call. However, his cries of pain didn't stop him joining me in downing two bottles of red wine. I slept really well that night, though it was a short one. As dawn broke, I got up to pee and found Nyima squatting in the dimly lit toilet taking a crap and reading a book.

6

As we carried on with our journey, he carried on with his stories, until the entire Qinghai–Tibet Highway became one long history lesson.

For instance, yesterday, when we saw rat holes, he told me that when the Chinese soldiers arrived in Tibet, they were so hungry they ate rats. They drove them out of the holes by pouring water in, or smoking them out, or using sheepskin bellows to blast air in.

'You mean the PLA Eighteenth Army?' I asked. 'My granddad worked as a labourer for the Eighteenth Army.'

But Nyima corrected me: 'To be accurate, it was troops controlled by the North-West Bureau of the Party that entered Tibet through Kokonor.

'We only ever talk about how disciplined the Eighteenth Army was when it arrived to "protect Tibet" and how peaceful the Liberation was and so on and so forth,' he went on. 'No one ever asks why, just a few years later, there was an uprising against Chinese rule in Kham and the two sides were at each other's throats. A lot of people have forgotten that there was resistance to collectivization in Kokonor in 1958, and that Chinese and Mongolian PLA soldiers massacred so many Tibetans that the population of some areas dropped by thirty or forty per cent.'

We were fifty kilometres past Golmud, getting to the Tsaidam Basin, and he told me about Nuo Mu Hong Farm, a dozen or so kilometres off the highway in an oasis. It produced the best wolfberries, he said, even better than Ningxia wolfberries. Before that, it used to be a prison farm and, before that, the land had been cleared and planted by demobbed Chinese soldiers. 'You have to give it to them, they had a rough time of it. For some reason best known to the authorities, they were plonked in the Gobi Desert in this remote spot.'

I asked: 'Were they like those Chinese volunteers who helped develop Tibet? They were willing to put up with any amount of hardship.'

'Something like that,' said Nyima. 'You have to give it to them . . .'

When we got to the Daotang River, he told me about the Tang Dynasty Princess Wencheng, who cried so hard on her way to Tibet that her tears made the river turn around and flow westwards with her, so they called it Turn-around River. King Trisong Detsen had threatened the Chinese emperor that if he didn't agree to give his daughter in marriage, he would personally lead 50,000 troops into China, kill the emperor and take his daughter by force. After much to-ing and fro-ing, the Chinese monarch finally agreed to send his daughter to Tibet. 'Yes, I know about that,' I said. 'We were invincible in those days, we even occupied Chang'an, the Tang Dynasty capital. Our king had lots of wives. Princess Wencheng was just one of them.'

I realized that Nyima was very particular about the language he used. He used the Mongolian name, Kokonor, instead of the Chinese, Qinghai. And he didn't talk, like the government did, about the 'Tibetan ethnic minority' or, worse still, 'Tubo barbarians'. He pronounced all the names the Tibetan way. When it came to places, he said 'Amdo' or 'Kham' or 'Dbus-Gtsang' and he was precise about people: they were from Shigatse, or from Lhasa or wherever. He talked about King Songtsen Gampo, the great emperor of the Bodpa dynasty. We were not 'Tibetans', the word the Chinese used, Nyima said. We were Bodpa, the ancient people of Bod.

7

It wouldn't take us long to get from Lake Kokonor to Xining that morning. Nyima was obviously ready with a new story. As soon as we got in the car, he burst out with: 'Huangzhong County! You know about this place, don't you?'

'Sure,' I said. 'It's near Xining. That's where the Kumbum Monastery is. We'll be there soon.'

'But do you know what happened there?'

'No, but I can see you're going to tell me.'

'Cannibalism.'

'How come I never saw that on the news?' I said, surprised. 'When was it?'

'During the Great Famine, the five years between 1958 and 1962.'

'Oh, then!' I said. 'That was ages ago. But I never heard about that. Did it really happen?'

'Of course it did,' said Nyima. 'There are documents to prove it. You can find stuff about it on the web. The thing is, do you really want to know the truth?'

'So what did happen, then?' I asked.

'Well, it was catastrophic. In 1960 alone, 12.87 per cent of the local population died, sometimes whole villages, and that's according to government documents. And there are at least three hundred recorded cases of cannibalism in this area alone. Some people ate corpses; in other cases they murdered then ate them. In one family, all nine children were eaten. Take Doba Township, for instance – hey, don't we pass by Doba on this road? Anyway, what happened in Doba was tragic, the population was almost wiped out. And Doba's only fifty kilometres from Xining.'

'Did they run out of food and die of starvation?' I asked.

'Yes, some starved to death,' Nyima said. 'And some died of disease because they were weakened from being half starved, and others were executed because their hunger made them disobey orders.'

'Did the crops fail?'

'Not all five years. Successive crop failures would be very unusual and most times the peasants don't starve from just one year of poor crops. Actually, in 1958 there was a bumper harvest.'

'Were all the deaths Tibetans?'

'Around Huangzhong it was mostly Chinese, not Tibetans.'

'The Chinese didn't have enough to eat either?'

'That's right. The disaster affected all the ethnic groups – Han Chinese, Tibetans and Hui Muslims alike. In those five years, there were over twenty million deaths countrywide from non-natural causes. Some people say it was double that, most of them, of course, Han Chinese.'

'Do you care what happened to the Chinese as well as the Tibetans?' I asked.

'Well, if they mess up, then the Tibetans and other national groups are going to have a hard time too.'

'But why didn't the government send aid? Maybe they didn't know what was going on.'

Nyima looked despairing at my ignorance. 'How could they have not known for five years on the trot? Huangzhong is right near Xining City, and Doba is only fifty kilometres away. In 1961, Wang Zhao, who was then the central government deputy head of Public Security, came to Qinghai and he asked the central authorities for disaster relief grain. Mao Zedong found out and during the Cultural Revolution, another five years on, had Wang Zhao put to death.'

'How do you know so much?' I asked.

'Well, I like collecting figures for premature deaths,' said Nyima. 'If you really want to know, you can find anything out. Is there anyone born in the 1940s and '50s in your family?'

'My gran. She lives in Shigatse.'

'In Shigatse? Collectivization started late in the Tibet Autonomous Region, and in places like Shigatse things weren't as bad as elsewhere, but still, ask your gran, and she'll tell you. The places which really suffered were Kham and Amdo, they collectivized at the same time as the rest of China. My family's from Sertar county in Sichuan province, where one-quarter of the population died between 1958 and 1960. In general, wherever you were, it was the peasants who died. In other words, it was the ones who tilled the soil who starved to death. Preposterous, isn't it! So how could it possibly have been a natural disaster? Generally speaking, people in town were better off than in the countryside; they went hungry but they didn't starve. Then, in 1978, there was drought all over China. Right at that time, the local government in a poor part of Anhui province decided to break up the communes and give the land back to individual families. I hardly need tell you that, in spite of the drought, no one starved and, in less than a year, every family had enough to eat. Catastrophic famines always have a human cause.'

My head was beginning to spin. 'You really are interested in death,' was all I could think of to say.

'I'm not interested in death *per se*,' said Nyima. 'I'm interested in evil. People lack imagination when it comes to evil. They never imagine that evil is really that evil . . .'

This conversation could go on for ever, I knew, so I deliberately didn't take him up on that.

Before we said goodbye, he took out a small notebook and jotted down my mobile number. Was there really anyone left in the world who didn't take their mobile with them every time they stepped out of the house?

Actually, after I'd dropped Nyima at Xining, I felt relaxed in a way I couldn't put into words. Straightaway, I put a Jay Chou track on.

8

I knew the section of Highway 109 between Lhasa and Xining like the back of my hand, I'd done it so often. But this would be the first time I carried on to Beijing. Last time, when Plum and I drove the Range Rover from Beijing back to Lhasa, I took the southern route through Xi'an and only joined the 109 at Xining. This time I was setting myself a challenge – to do the entire Beijing–Lhasa Highway. It would take me via Lanzhou, Yinchuan, the Ordos desert and Da Tong, the kilometre markers going down and down as I drove.

I don't normally drive into cities, it's a waste of time and you get snarled up in traffic. So I took the ring roads, and found places to sleep on the outskirts or in small towns. Past Yinchuan, I spent one night in a small guesthouse run by Hui Muslims. Now I'd got this far, I could plan the last two days' journey. It wouldn't be fast driving. From here to Da Tong via the Ordos was not far but it was a coal-mining area and I would get held up by the lorries. I figured I'd do a short stretch tomorrow.

I didn't want to get to Beijing at night. I planned to stay the last night somewhere near Da Tong so I could be sure of getting into Beijing around midday the next day.

That last day, I drove through three provinces. You just had to keep going. The national highway had become a coal-transport route. Heavily laden lorries hogged the road, there were open-face mines everywhere, and the air was thick with dust.

The sun never came out all day.

Once in Shanxi province, I was in the heartland of China. On the outskirts of Da Tong, I stopped at what looked like a decent-sized guesthouse but at Reception the clerk fetched the manager and they spent a long time poring over my ID card, before telling me they didn't have a room for me. Why not? It was discrimination, pure and simple.

I was angry and I was hungry. I turned on the 3G wireless router and got on to Booking.com on the iPad. Then I used my credit card to book a room at the 5-star Holiday Inn in the city centre.

This trip had been very eventful. I thought I'd taken it all in my stride, but some things were bothering me, all the same. I didn't feel like eating meat, or playing computer games, and I even seemed to have repressed my sexual fantasies. My head was full of death. That was not like me at all. Maybe it was to do with going so far away from people and places I knew and the life I was used to. Lhasa, with its blue skies and sunshine, was a long way behind me. Now was my chance to transform my life. I was actually a bit scared. I needed a good rest now. I'd drive into Beijing tomorrow.

Chapter Four

1

WHEN I FINALLY got to Beijing, the Range Rover was filthy from the journey so I went to a car wash. Up till now, I'd followed my plan to the letter. What next?

It occurred to me to turn round and drive right back to Lhasa. I'd pretend I'd taken a trip to Shigatse or something, then return to Plum, casual as you please, and take up the good life where I'd left off.

But I couldn't go back to Lhasa. Only Beijing and Shell could save me. Once I got to the western outskirts of the city, I brought up the GPS map and found a drive-in car wash. In the tunnel, the high-pressure jets of water sprayed the car, then it got a foam shampoo, then it was buffed by an enormous brush at the end of a robotic arm, waxed, and finally blow-dried.

Driving this morning, I had a hard-on several times. But the big guy knew quite well that the little guy was excited about nothing. Just because we'd got to Beijing, it didn't mean that Beijing was going to roll out the red carpet. This little guy was an arsehole. The big guy was an arsehole too . . . what on earth made me think Shell would pay any attention to me?

In the end it was the touchscreen on my mobile which made the decision for me. I was looking at Shell's number, half of me longing to call her, the other half not daring to – when suddenly I heard a ring tone and Shell's voice answering: 'Hello? Hello? Is that Champa? Can you hear me?'

I pulled myself together and tried to sound calm. 'Shell, yes, this is Champa, I'm in Beijing.'

'Hello! How are you? Is my mum with you?'

'Plum's in Burma,' I told her. 'I've come on my own.'

'Oh. Whereabouts in Beijing are you?'

'The western edge of the sixth ring road, near the extension of Chang'an Avenue,' I said, looking at the GPS.

'You drove, did you?'

'Yep. I'm driving now. I'd like to meet you—'

'That would be great! Go round the sixth ring road to the east side, I'm heading there myself. I'll text you the precise location but, for the moment, look for the Zhangjiawan Road section, we're meeting there, all the volunteers are going. I've got to take another call now, I'll text you in a bit and we can meet there.' And she rang off.

I put the phone down then put it back to my ear again. 'Right, we'll meet there in a bit.' Yay! Gimme five!

2

We've found a huge lorry loaded with dogs. Sixth ring road, Zhangjiawan Road section.

Hebei R registration.

It's taken the Beijing–Harbin Expressway.

Zi An, is Yang with you?

Yang's driving, we're following the lorry.

We drove past and took a look. God, it's terrible, it's stuffed full of dogs!

We counted, twelve cages stacked four high, 12 times 4 makes 48, times six is nearly three hundred dogs.

Yang says it's more than three hundred. It's 48 cages times 10.

Yang says we've got to cut the lorry off, but I'm scared.

Good god! There are all kinds of dogs . . . big tan farm guard dogs, golden retrievers, huskies, Labradors, Samoyeds, greyhounds, chows, Alsatians, hunting hounds, golden mastiffs, Pyrenean mountain dogs.

Oh god! Lots of them have collars on.

They must be stolen.

Of course they're stolen.

Stolen.

They must be taking them for slaughter.

To be turned into dog meat.

Are all dogs for eating stolen?

No one has dog farms any more. If they didn't steal them, where would they get them from?

Why don't people have dog farms?

It's too expensive to raise big dogs. You don't get much per pound of dog meat.

In the south-west, dogs are still farmed for meat. They eat dogs, and some places hold dog meat festivals.

It's not economical to raise dogs for meat, so the business depends on stealing them.

The dog-meat supply chain depends on the dog-theft business.

Mostly they steal farm guard dogs because they're not kept chained up.

They steal town dogs too.

They use bitches to attract the males.

They use blow-darts and poisoned buns.

That's so cruel.

We can't let them get away with it.

We've got to think of a way of saving the dogs.

Report them to the police.

Yang's shouting at the lorry driver to stop.

He's taking no notice, I'm scared.

Yang's cutting the lorry up.

She nearly hit it.

She's not going to make it! The lorry's going too fast. I'm so scared.

Yang, stop doing that!

Tell Yang to stop it.

You should tell the police.

Zi An, tell Yang I've reported it to the police.

I have too.

We've sent a group text.

This is Shell. I'm nearly there! Hold on!

We're in front of the lorry now, we're slowing it down.

That's dangerous.

Be careful.

The lorry's trying to pass but we're blocking it.

Yang, watch he doesn't run into you.

The lorry driver's indicating.

He's pulled into the kerb.

We're stopped near exit 25 of the Beijing–Harbin highway.

Yang's got out.

There are three men in the lorry.

I'm going to see Yang. No more chatting. Come as quick as you can.

Get there quick and rescue Zi An and Yang.

Pet Friends got the text and forwarded.

Pet Guards got the text and forwarded.

I Love My Dog know, and forwarded.

Appointment with Dogs got the text.

Feline Friends League got the text and support you.

Students for Compassion are following and forwarded.

The Stray Dogs Alliance is on its way.

Human Love is mobilizing.

Rainbow World is launching into action.

Shell, did you tell the Animal Protection League?

Yes, they're reporting it to the Beijing Municipal Bureau of Agriculture right now.

Everyone, get there as quick as you can!

I'm already on the 6th ring road east side.

I'm on the 5th ring road, heading towards the 6th.

Zi An's OK, is she?

Any news about Zi An and Yang?

None.

This is the Tongzhou district police. We've seen your tweets, please tell us the exact spot.

Near exit 25 of the Beijing–Harbin highway, look for a white Merc and a lorry with a Hebei province R registration.

I can see it. Thanks for that.

What's going to happen now?

There's a cop car on the scene.

That's good!

Tell Yang, I can see you both and the cops.

I can see them.

I'm almost there.

I'm on the opposite side of the expressway. I can see loads of dogs. It's horrible the way they're cooped up in there.

It's so cruel.

Everyone take water and give the dogs a drink.

I've got bottled water, dog food, glucose and saline drips. I'm on my way now.

I can see Yang, Zi An and Shell arguing with the dog trader.

The cops are there.

One dog's bleeding. Another one looks like it's dead.

One of the bitches has a prolapsed womb.

Another's got a broken tail and it's maggotty.

Are there any vets at the scene?

There are several dead dogs.

My boyfriend's a vet, and I've told him to get himself there.

I'm a surgeon, and I'll be there soon.

They're moving off. They say they're going to park up at the Kuo Xian tollbooths.

The cops want everyone on the tollbooth slip road so they don't block the carriageway.

Now they're saying only the lorry and Yang's car can go through, we can't go.

Shell's having an argument with the cops.

They've agreed we can send representatives. Shell's gone in Yang's car, the lorry's left too.

And Dan Dan's gone. We have to stay on the expressway.

Do we have a lawyer?

Seven more cars of volunteers have arrived.

They say they're going to cordon off the area so no one else can get near the dogs.

I work in a law firm, but I'm stuck on the 5th ring road.

I'm a lawyer, I'll be there soon.

At least twenty vehicles have turned up.

Shell's demanding that the cops let us give the dogs a drink first. They've agreed. Two at a time.

Apparently the police want nothing to do with lorries which are just passing through. Shell wanted me to pass on the message.

The dog trader says he got the inspection certificate from another province.

He can't have been through the safety checks.

Do stolen dogs get a certificate?!

Bribery and corruption!

They're demanding to see the safety certificate.

If he's really got his certificate, won't they have to let him go?

I'm afraid they can't stop him.

They absolutely mustn't let him go. That's sending the dogs to their deaths.

They're saying there are 520 dogs on that lorry.

That'll be a massacre.

If we let the lorry go, the blood will be on our hands.

Please don't let the dogs be bludgeoned to death or have their throats cut . . . they'll be so terrified.

I've counted. We've got over thirty volunteer cars here now.

I swear we're going to save those dogs.

A lot of cop cars have turned up.

Why so many?

I've done nothing wrong, I'm not scared of the police.

You know what to say: 'Do you know who I am, officer?!'

I'm a volunteer, I've worked in the courts. We mustn't wind the cops up. Our aim is to save the dogs.

Saving the dogs comes first.

We've got to find a way to stop the lorry leaving.

Get all the volunteers over here to block the lorry.

We've got over fifty cars. No way is that lorry leaving.

Tell the police the dogs are stolen.

There's no proof.

Their collars.

The dog trader says the breeders forgot to take the collars off when he bought them.

What rubbish! Barefaced liar!

Transporting dogs like that is mistreatment.

Mistreatment is not against the law.

China has no laws on mistreatment.

People who mistreat dogs should rot in hell.

People who eat pets should rot in hell.

People who eat companion animals should rot in hell.

Please everyone calm down. Let's get back to theft and food safety issues.

Everyone stop arguing. Let's think of a way of saving the dogs.

I'm uploading pictures of some of the dogs, but it's very slow.

The Agricultural Bureau quarantine inspectors are here, they're looking at the documentation.

The dogs are being transported from Henan to Jilin where they'll be slaughtered.

They're saying the certificate and the stamp's genuine.

That's not possible.

You can buy certificates and stamps.

Even if the certificate's genuine, it doesn't mean the safety check was done.

Damned corrupt officials!

I'm from Zhengzhou. My Labrador's been gone for days. I just happen to be in Beijing right now, and I'm on my way over. Whatever you do don't let the lorry go. Please, I beg you, save my dog.

Bad news: the Beijing Animal Hygiene inspectors have verified that the quarantine certificates and the animal products transport disinfection certificates were issued by their Luoyang counterparts and they're all legit.

That's it, then.

What are we going to do? Those dogs will die.

I'm getting my mum to contact the Beijing Municipal Party Committee.

Yang and Shell have told the police we're not letting the lorry go. Everyone do what you think best.

What does that mean?

If we don't let it go, what will the cops do?

Yang and Shell are so great . . .

We'll make such a fuss if they're let go, then we'll see who's afraid of whom.

Which cops are these?

Tongzhou district. Do you know anyone there?

We'll block the lorry so it can't leave.

Right, we mustn't back down.

Beijing pet protection volunteers stick together!

There are at least eighty police now.

The cordon stretches a hundred metres.

We should go in and rescue the dogs, or at least as many as we can.

Calm down. The two girls, Yang and Shell, are still negotiating.

Who's in charge here? I'd like to be in on the negotiations.

I'm A-Shan, from Storm Cat and Dog Rescue. We should have a bit of patience. We need to surround the lorry so it can't leave, but not provoke a confrontation.

We should wait and see the outcome of Yang and Shell's negotiations.

Support A-Shan!

Whatever you do, don't create an incident and provoke the police.

We can't give them an excuse to get rid of us.

We should simply surround them and watch, but we must keep our distance.

Well said.

You people who've just arrived, quieten down.

Anyone who wants to feed and water the dogs, please report to Wang Dajun, from Companion Animals, in the red and white pickup truck.

The media are here, both the press and online reporters.

I'll go and brief them.

Anyone who's had media experience, meet by the red and white pickup.

The dog trader's agreed to let sick dogs off the lorry so they can be treated.

That's good.

But only five dogs.

That's not good enough.

They've let two Happy Home volunteers in to pick the five most seriously ill dogs.

One's lost a lot of blood, we can see that from here. It's the bitch with the prolapsed womb, she needs help.

If it's a prolapsed womb, it would be a bitch, wouldn't it?

Yang and Shell want every organization here to send one delegate to a meeting.

Why don't we raise the money and buy the dogs?

Yes, buy the lot.

I disagree. Why should we fork out our own money?

Some of the dogs are dead. The whole lorry should be subject to another hygiene inspection.

We can't let the dog trader make a profit.

If we don't buy the dogs, the lorry will leave.

All the representatives can go inside the police cordon and report to Zi An and Dan Dan.

Is there anyone from the Benevolent Fund for Animal Welfare here? Yang and Shell are looking for you.

Please everyone be patient. We just have to wait for the delegates' decision.

The police have agreed that the lorry can't leave until we've finished our meeting.

If they dare drive off, we'll be right on their tail. We'll hunt them down till we find them.

One mobile and one watch with a white leather strap have been found. If you've lost one, please ask Mrs Qing from the Fragrance Dogs Home. She's in the black Audi next to the red and white pickup.

3

I got a text from Shell: 'Exit 25, Beijing–Harbin Expressway.'

I was OK with reading Chinese characters but not used to writing them. I wasn't too good at the western alphabet either, so I couldn't write Chinese in *pinyin* very well. Right now, I was sorry that I didn't have WeChat on my mobile.

When I got to the highway, I called Shell's number a few times, but it was always engaged. I wrote 'Zai na?' Where are you? But there was no answer.

It didn't take long to get to exit 25. There was a line of cars a kilometre long parked at the roadside. I could see a load of police cars and dozens of police, some of them keeping the traffic flowing. I parked up two hundred metres from the exit. The other cars were a mixture of fancy imported models and ordinary Chinese-made cars . . . lots of 4x4s, plus saloons, commercial vehicles, sports cars, and a red and white pickup. More cars were turning up as I watched. I couldn't see Shell.

There were over a hundred people on the exit slip road. Most were young but there were a few middle-aged ones too. There were girls and guys. Some wore combat gear, others were in suits and ties, but most had jeans on, like I did. Some looked obviously gay or lesbian. Some of the faces were familiar – maybe they were famous artists.

Everyone was standing around outside the police cordon, smoking, or looking at their mobiles or iPads. It was all quite orderly. Inside the cordon, I saw a white Merc, a van from some Beijing municipal department, two police cars and an enormous lorry loaded up with dogs. Shell was inside the cordon.

I followed the cordon, trying to catch Shell's eye but she was too busy issuing commands to the group through her mobile or passing messages to other women, just like a young commander, like her mother in fact. I got as close to her as I could and took her picture with my mobile.

One of the police thought I was taking his photo and glared at me: 'What do you think you're doing?'

Shell came over. 'What's up? He's one of our volunteers.' The policeman looked scared of annoying Shell and, with a muttered 'It's nothing', walked away.

I stood right next to the cordon. The road surface was pot-holed where I was, and Shell stumbled as she came over and grabbed my arm to steady herself. She leaned over to whisper: 'They got the safety documents. The police'll have to let them leave. We've decided to buy the dogs. We're collecting donations. The dog trader is asking too much so we're dragging our feet. That way, he'll get worried and drop his price. Our volunteers and the Agricultural Bureau people are making a head count. We won't be paying for the sick and the dead ones. We've got a few tricks up our sleeve . . .'

I felt her breath against my ear, and hardly dared breathe.

'How are you for time?' she asked me.

'I don't have anything on,' I said. 'I just came to see you.'

'This might go on pretty late,' she whispered. 'We'll need cars later. Can we use yours?'

'Sure,' I said. 'It's back there.'

She let go of my arm and stepped back. 'Can you use the web on your phone?'

I showed her: 'It's 3G.' She took it from me.

'Have you got WeChat?'

'No.'

'Keep an eye on Zi An's tweets,' she told me. 'That'll give you an idea of what's going on.' She typed in '@ZiAn' and gave the phone back to me. 'I'm going back there, you have a read of this.'

Shell walked over to the white Mercedes, then turned and gave me a mischievous wink. Dammit, that was the Tara's bright gaze and Plum's naughty expression.

I read Zi An's tweets and comments but didn't find them particularly interesting. Before it got dark, some of the volunteers handed out food and drinks. I ate mine, and someone came round with a big bag for rubbish.

I got a text from Shell: 'Champa, can you drive your car over to where Wang Dajun is, by the red and white pickup?'

I drove up to the pickup and found Dajun. He was one of the ones in combat gear. 'Are you Champa?' he asked. 'Can you take Feng and these four dogs to the veterinary hospital?'

The volunteers loaded four very dirty dogs into the back seat of my car. I didn't dare look round – just the stink of them told me more than enough.

As we drove along, Feng told me that they'd discovered a dozen corpses during their head count and fifty or sixty sick dogs. The dog trader had agreed to let thirty of the sickest go and these were being taken to different vets.

I left Feng and the dogs at a vet's surgery in Chaoyang district and drove back to exit 25. There were even more people than before and a bunch of reporters filming and taking pictures. Back at the red and white pickup, I asked Dajun what he'd like me to do next. He whispered in my ear: 'We're still haggling him down. We're nearly there.'

'Have we got enough money?' I asked.

He dropped his voice even lower: 'Yes, we've raised enough but the man doesn't know that.'

Then he asked, as if he was conferring a great honour on me: 'Would you like to feed the dogs?'

'Fine,' I said.

'OK, the next round, you go.'

A quarter of an hour later, I was walking around the lorry with other volunteers, passing food and water into the cages. Their occupants had been cooped up in horrible conditions all day and the cages were swimming in blood and excrement and stank to high heaven. In the dim torchlight, I could see a girl next to me. She was engrossed in attending to the dogs, reaching out so that her top rode up and showed her bare back. Her clothes were soaked in dog slobber. I fed them too, as gently as I could.

Shell came up to me: 'You're not afraid of dogs, are you, Champa?'

'Of course not!' I said. 'I just don't like it when people say I give dogs a bad name.'

Shell looked startled. Then she put her palms together beseechingly: 'I'm so sorry, Champa, I really am!'

'It doesn't matter,' I said. 'This voluntary dog duty's my punishment!'

She smiled and moved away.

Plum called but I didn't pick up. I didn't want to keep telling her I was in Shigatse, but I also didn't dare tell her the truth. I turned my phone off.

4

It took until eleven o'clock at night for the dog trader to agree on 110,000 *yuan*, and by the time the money had been paid over, it was after midnight. The cars escorted the lorry to the Small and Medium-sized Animals Sanctuary at Bei'anhe to the west of Beijing. This was a centre for strays, municipal-government-approved so it could legally raise funds. It was also the only place big enough to take so many.

Shell had turned up in one of those made-in-China Skoda Fabias that you saw everywhere, and now she drove herself away in it. I followed.

At the sanctuary, everyone got busy recording several hundred dogs. The lorry men made a fuss about wanting to get on their way so the workers released all the dogs at once. It was mayhem – hundreds of dogs jumping down and running madly around barking – and almost impossible to carry on listing them. Some owners who'd lost their dogs had come along with us. One of them had even flown in from Luoyang that afternoon, and another was the woman from Zhengzhou who just happened to be in Beijing, but they hadn't managed to locate their own dogs yet. The lorry driver took the money and drove off.

Another task was to bury the dead ones. The old woman in charge of the Animals Sanctuary asked for volunteers to dig graves. I noticed that all the well-muscled hunks had mysteriously disappeared and I reckoned I was pretty fit so I joined a little group and we dug until three in the morning.

Shell came over to get me. She said that some of the pet protection groups including hers were taking the dozens of sick and injured dogs with them. There turned out to be far more than we thought – you only saw their injuries properly in the electric light. I wondered why this place couldn't look after them. Shell said they were more than willing to. The more dogs they had, the more money the old woman could raise. Now that the news had got out about today's incident and the fact that the dogs had been sent here, lots of public figures would cough up contributions. But the old woman and her staff simply couldn't cope with the badly injured ones and the volunteers decided to take advantage of the chaos and confusion and take them away for proper treatment and care, rather than leave them to die here.

Three big dogs with obvious injuries were put into my car. Go right ahead, I thought to myself, dogs, this car belongs to you, any injured ones can sit in it, I'm honoured!

We drove in convoy to the Happy Home dogs home the girls ran in Tongzhou Village – Yang and Zi An in their Merc, Shell in her Skoda and me in the Range Rover.

The lights were on at the Happy Home dogs home, and a hundred or so dogs yapped and barked excitedly at our arrival. I saw a banner which read: 'Let living creatures stray no longer.'

The caretakers were a middle-aged couple from the village, Old Li and his wife. We cleared out some small, covered pens to put the sick dogs in. The fighting dogs were put in a medium-sized open-air pen and the rest, the ones that would get on with other dogs, all went into the biggest open-air enclosure. Two were penned individually – one was half crazy, the other vicious. Stray cats were in another large pen. Ringing the compound were half a dozen shacks. From one of them, used for storing the animal feed and bits and pieces, we pulled out some old blankets, put some on the floor of the sick dogs' pens and hung the rest over the railings of the open-air pens to keep out the cold air.

Yang and Zi An left before daybreak. Shell asked: 'Where are you staying in Beijing?'

'Nowhere yet,' I said.

'Then let's go and kip down in there,' she pointed, and I followed her over to a building.

'Wait, I've got something for you,' I said. And I went to get the Tara figurine, wrapped in its *khata*, out of the back of the car and brought it inside.

Shell turned on the fan heater, took a couple of blankets out of the cupboard and rolled them flat on the two single bedsteads.

I put the Tara on the table. Suddenly Shell asked: 'Is that why you came to Beijing?'

'Yes,' I said, then, ' . . . no. It wasn't quite like that. I actually came to see you.'

She paused a moment, then said softly: 'Really?'

'Yes, really.'

'Why?'

My heart skipped a beat and I didn't know what to say. I hadn't written that into the script.

To my surprise, she came straight out with it: 'You really care about me?'

'Yes! I really care about you.'

She stood stock still, conflicting feelings showing in her face, then turned, went into the toilet and shut the door.

I had no idea what to do. I just stood there. Time went by and Shell didn't come out. I opened the door and went out. It was very dark outside, and cold, so I came back in pretty quickly.

I sat down on an old sofa and must have dozed off. I woke up to find someone stroking my face. Shell was bending over me, her soft hand on my face. I grabbed hold of her and pulled her on top of me.

I kissed her and she let me. I put my hand inside her clothes, inside her bra, and her breasts were just as I had imagined, little and pointy like steamed cornbreads but not hard, soft and light. I undid her trouser buttons and she undid my belt and unzipped me. We stripped each other off, she took my cock and put it into her tight little cunt. I yelped, and she clamped her hand over my mouth to keep me quiet. She got on top of me and gently rocked back and forth, gripping my shoulders hard, raising herself up a bit, then pushing back in again. Twice, I wanted to roll on top of her but she pinned me down. She rocked back and forth and from side to side, completely focused on directing my cock so that it pressed against her G spot. I watched her eyes glaze over and an expression almost of pain on her face. What was going through her mind? I had no idea. But my little guy was angry now! My eyeballs were popping out and my cock felt like it was bursting. A jolt of lightning ran through me and suddenly I was on fire.

PART THREE

Alien Land

Chapter Five

1

BEIJING WELCOMES you . . . Beijing welcomes you . . . the Olympics jingle was going round and round in my head. In my semi-conscious state, it sounded really weird. Beijing welcomes you . . . Beijing welcomes you . . .

I can't have slept much more than an hour. I woke to see Shell sitting on a chair, already dressed. Her eyes were half closed but when she noticed I was awake, she jumped to her feet. 'I'm off!' she said.

I sat up but she stopped me:

'You have a bit more sleep. I've got a meeting in town this morning, at an advertising company. They're giving me a job and I need to go home first to pick up stuff, so I'll be off now.' She sounded like she'd rehearsed her explanation.

She paused, then said more quietly: 'If you want to leave, just shut the door behind you.'

I didn't say anything. I was puzzling over what she meant.

She went to the door, then went on: 'If you decide to stay, the volunteers will be here in a bit, you could help them and Mr and Mrs Li with the dogs. I'll be back this evening.'

She seemed on the point of saying something more, looked at

me, then said: 'If you don't go . . . then you'd better give Mum a ring.'

Still bemused, I went to the window and watched Shell drive away in her Skoda. It was daylight but the sky was overcast. Outside, there was only the row of shacks to be seen and, in the far distance, a few skyscrapers. Was I really in Beijing?

Shell had given me the chance to shut the door behind me and go. Was this just a one-night stand? I could go straight back to Lhasa. Shell had given me a chance to back out. This was my very last chance to put into reverse the great life change I'd planned for myself. After this, there'd be no going back, ever.

Why had I come to Beijing? At the very least, I'd come for sex, even if it was only for one night. Now I didn't have that craving any more. Instead, I had another, very clear, feeling (and I was someone who always trusted my feelings). There was no way I wanted to go back to my former life. I wanted to begin my new life here, in Beijing. Shell would be my jumping-off point.

I was making my position clear simply by not leaving, there was no need to say any more.

Beijing welcomes you . . . Beijing welcomes you . . . I looked at my phone. There were seven or eight missed calls. I sighed. I'm sorry, Plum. I really am. Beijing welcomes you . . . Beijing welcomes you . . .

I painfully input my text in *pinyin*:

'Plum, am in Beijing, not returning Lhasa. I've fallen in love, that's why I came to Beijing. Goodbye, Plum, I'm so, so sorry. And I'm so, so grateful to you too. Thank you, Plum. Champa.'

2

My granddad used to tell me: 'Learn to speak Chinese properly and you can go to Beijing.' When I was a kid, that was the reason why I liked speaking Chinese, so I could go to Beijing. My granddad had been a labourer for the Eighteenth Army, and one of the perks was a trip to Beijing. His Chinese wasn't that good, but he used to like saying he'd been invited to Beijing.

From the day I got my driver's licence, I was given the old family Xiali to drive. My dad said: 'Now you can drive your mum and dad to Beijing.' I never did take them, I never got the chance. In the next life, maybe.

I made a name for myself at middle school because of Beijing. Once, an elderly relative of my mother's came back to Lhasa from Switzerland. He asked me if I'd like to travel abroad. 'Sure!' I said. 'I want to go to Beijing.' The result was I got a lecture from him on the glories of Tibet's past: when the Jokhang Temple was built in Lhasa a thousand years ago, what did Beijing have? Nothing. A thousand years ago, all there was in China was the Tang dynasty, and their capital, Chang'An, used to belong to Tibet too. Beijing back in those days was nothing, what do you want to go there for? I got really upset then. First, I tried contradicting him, then he hit me and I hit him back. He gave me a terrible hiding for that, but he was an elderly gent and if it got around that he'd been scrapping with a teenager, he'd never live it down. I didn't care, in any case, and my mates at school thought I was the dog's bollocks. I remember that when we were pulled apart, he was practically apoplectic with rage, and carried on bellowing at me that Beijing was built by the Mongols and the Manchus, and our high lamas were their emperors' teachers.

Apparently, I swore back at him Beijing-style: 'That's fuck-all to do with me!' or something like that. At least that's what the neighbours say I said, but I'm not so sure, because in those days, I didn't know how to swear like that, the most I would have said was dammit or something like that. But after this, there was no holding me back. I made a name for myself with all my Beijing swearwords.

After that incident, my mates at school called me 'Beijing-fixated'. I strolled along Beijing Road, watched the Beijing Olympics on TV and ate Peking duck. My middle-school Chinese teacher was a

Beijinger. She was one of the last university students to be sent under the Support Tibet scheme.

I always wanted a girlfriend from Beijing. Every year, lots of Beijingers came on holiday to Lhasa and I learned plenty of Beijing slang off them. I used to walk like a Beijinger, talk like a Beijinger and dress like one too. I stopped acting like my dad; I reckoned he had an inferiority complex because my granddad had been a low-class blacksmith. But I could change and that gave me a very good opinion of myself. From my first year in middle school, I refused to wear the clothes my mum bought me any more. I mean, my mum and my two elder sisters were such bumpkins. I didn't want people to think I was one too.

Of course, I wasn't daft enough to say that everything from Beijing was good. It was just that stuff from Beijing always drew my attention. I'd stick up for Beijing in an argument, though I'd do the same for Lhasa too.

And after a few years with Plum, I was even more convinced that I was at least half a Beijinger.

And now I'd finally driven here. Driving myself all along Highway 109 from Lhasa to Beijing was the first step in realizing my dream. Mum, Dad, I did it! Beijing, here I come. Sorry I kept you waiting so long, Beijing. Beijing welcomes you . . . Beijing welcomes you . . . it was going round and round in my head like an earworm.

3

Plum might call at any moment and I didn't know what I would say. For sure, she'd tear me off a strip. I reckoned I'd just say 'I'm sorry'. Whatever names she called me, 'sorry' was all I could say . . .

But Plum didn't call. Maybe she hadn't got up yet or hadn't looked at her mobile.

I opened the Range Rover door. It stank of dogs. I couldn't be bothered to clean it out, so I just opened a window to air the inside.

Mr and Mrs Li gave me breakfast of rice porridge and told me there was some of yesterday's solar-heated water left, I could have a wash if I liked. So I went back to our room and took a shower in the ramshackle toilet cubicle.

Then two middle-aged women turned up, followed by an elderly couple. The volunteers took it in turns every morning to help Mr and Mrs Li with the dogs. They all knew what to do, getting the food ready, ladling it out, feeding and watering the cats and dogs, cleaning the pens and cages, washing the dogs and playing with the dogs and cats. There were nearly two hundred dogs, many of them maimed, I saw.

I was thinking about that call, the one that should have come, but hadn't, from Plum. I was worried sick. But Shell had asked me to help with the dogs so I'd better get on with it. The dogs ate, then crapped, and as soon as I saw one do that, I got the shovel. When the volunteers saw all the new arrivals, they started talking excitedly about yesterday's hold-up of the dog trader's lorry. I sidled up to them. 'I was there,' I told them. They plied me with questions and I began to cheer up. I talked volubly in Chinese and everyone became very enthusiastic. I began to feel I would get on just fine with these Beijingers.

The volunteers went off for lunch. I had a bowl of noodles with the Lis. Plum hadn't answered my text. I'd been dreading her call but her silence made me just as uneasy. I wondered if she hadn't received the text, or I'd written the Chinese wrong and hadn't made myself clear.

After lunch, Zi An and Yang came over in the Merc and we divided up the injured dogs between the cars and drove them to the Tongzhou Pampered Pets Clinic. The treatment was expensive, I could see, and Yang told me that volunteers paid out of their own pockets.

'Back to the kennels?' I asked when we'd finished.

'Back to the dogs home,' Zi An corrected me kindly.

'Right,' I said. 'It's not called the kennels, then.'

Later that afternoon, a lot of younger volunteers turned up, mostly girls. I gave them a hand inserting the dogs' microchips because it was hard work. Then they all clustered around Yang and Zi An and talked about yesterday. They were the heroines and the centre of attention. I hovered nearby but no one asked me anything. Then a young guy called Melon-head brought over three dogs so badly injured they probably needed operating on and told me to run them to the Yongkang Animal Hospital in Chaoyang. The traffic was snarled up both ways. I kept thinking about Plum's phone call – couldn't get it out of my mind so I told Melon-head I'd been there yesterday, and gave him the whole story, adding a lot more details. Melon-head got very enthused. He was a nice guy, said he'd got the nickname Melon-head because his friends reckoned he had a face like a winter melon. He turned out to be older than me, though he looked younger, and was a hospital nurse who did night shifts. He told me that, of the Beijing volunteer groups, the Happy Home Volunteers were especially well known for adopting strays who were maimed. There were over a hundred groups in the Beijing area that took in stray cats and dogs, he said, and there was an unofficial division of labour: A-Shan's Storm Cat and Dog Rescue specialized in rescuing the ones in difficulty, cats who'd got stuck at the top of a building and couldn't get down, or dogs who'd fallen into a hole and couldn't get out. Mrs Qing's Fragrance Dogs Home neutered stray cats and dogs, and Wang Dajun's Companion Animals organization held adoption days once a month so people could come and adopt a dog.

I asked him why Beijing had so many strays. It was to do with people abandoning their pets, he said. Especially with so much demolition and new building going on in the city – some people couldn't take their dogs when they got rehoused and left them behind.

Lhasa used to have a stray dog problem too, I told him, and

they were scaring the tourists off, so there was a big cull and there were fewer of them now. Melon-head said they were against culling. They thought the best way was neutering strays. After that, they could be adopted into new homes or be looked after in the volunteer-run dogs homes.

'I know,' I said. '"Let living creatures stray no longer" . . . that's what you believe, isn't it?'

'Yes,' he said, 'plus . . . adoption not trade, and neutering not culling.'

Plum still hadn't called.

4

It was the peak of the afternoon rush hour and it took over an hour to get back from Chaoyang to Tongzhou. I followed the GPS, but it kept directing me on to very snarled-up roads. I was fretting a bit but Melon-head just said I was getting a taste of the usual Beijing traffic jams.

I was fretting because Plum hadn't called, and because Shell might get back to the kennels before me and, when she saw my car wasn't there, she might think I really had shut the door behind me and left, and then how would she feel? My heart ached at the thought.

It was getting dark by the time we arrived. As I drove in and parked, Shell trotted over to the railings around the car park and waited for me to get out. I walked over to her and, under the streetlights, I could see she was agitated. I was agitated too. We stood on either side of the railings and looked at each other. She said nothing, just half lifted her right hand in greeting. I did the same, and she smiled. Then she turned and went back to the dogs.

That evening, the place was full of volunteers eating, chatting, all reading the tweets and reports about the rescue on their iPads or mobiles. The news had spread all around China and was one of the twittersphere's ten hot topics of the day.

One by one, the volunteers trickled off and I went back to our room. I looked at my mobile. Plum still hadn't called me. That must mean she'd got my text, otherwise she'd have carried on calling me for sure. So after she got the text, why hadn't she called me back? Maybe she was busy and would call tonight. I hoped that when she did, Shell would be here with me, to boost my confidence.

Shell hung around until everyone had left the kennels and the Lis had gone home, before coming back to the shack where we were sleeping.

She shut the door and leaned against it, looking down with an embarrassed smile and avoiding my eyes. But when I went up to her, she put her arms around me and kissed me. I carried her to the bed, laid her down and began to undress her. 'Wait, wait!' she said and stood up to get a small packet of condoms out of her backpack. The cellophane packaging was hard to remove and she picked at it for ages. As she crouched on the floor and worked away at the package, it struck me that this girl had gone to buy condoms without even knowing if I'd still be here when she got back. I imagined her feeling all knotted up inside, and a wave of excitement swept over me.

She put a condom on me. The sight of my cock made her giggle, for some reason, like it was comical, or the action of putting on the condom was funny, or new and strange. But I already knew she was sexually experienced. Surely this wasn't the first time she'd put a condom on a man? 'What are you laughing at?' I asked. She didn't answer. We knelt on the bed facing each other, and I peeled off her top and played with her nipples. She avoided my eyes, and giggled shyly. She hadn't been shy last night, so why was she being so coy today?

I was just getting on top of her when she asked: 'Did you talk to her?'

'Yes!' I said.

5

We lay naked in each other's arms on the single bed. I was so happy. I looked at the Tara sitting on the desk and said: 'It really looks like you.'

'Of course it does!' said Shell. 'I used a photo of myself to make it different from the traditional Tara.'

'You designed it yourself?'

'Part of it. I did three years' computer design at college. My mother thought I'd like it if she asked me to remodel a Tara. She even paid me a design fee. So I took a picture of myself and made the face a bit rounder. I imagined Mum on her knees to me all day – hilarious!'

'Bad girl,' I said.

'Just a little bit. But honestly, I didn't think she'd ever use my design.'

'Is it OK to change how the Tara looks then?'

'Of course. I found this out from a book by Amdo Champa, the Tibetan *thangka* artist, and when he paints the Tara, he uses live models. I don't have the money to pay models so all I had to go on was myself.'

'So the Tara's breasts were modelled on your own?'

'You've really got an eye for the girls. You even spotted that.'

I told her, slightly embarrassed, that I was an expert in the shape of female breasts.

'I think you've positioned them a bit too high though,' I said.

'That was Amdo Champa. He said you shouldn't make her too realistic. Realism is vulgar. So he deliberately raised the nipple line by ten centimetres. It would make her seem more spiritual, he said.'

'I think it's made her more sexy,' I said.

6

There was a frenzy of barking outside and I surfaced from a dream about a bear hunting me for its dinner. A car raced into the compound, headlights glaring.

There was a violent bang on the door and three men burst in.

I stood up, naked except for the rug I had wrapped around my hips.

One man, who looked Central Asian, seemed delighted to find me there and grinned, baring two rose-gold-capped teeth. 'Come here!' he beckoned.

I shook my head. 'Who are you?' I asked.

At that, Gold Teeth leapt at me. I raised my fists to defend myself but he got in first and landed a blow on the right side of my ribs. It hurt like hell. I let the rug slip and sat down heavily on the bed. The other two hoisted me to my feet and pressed down on my head. Then they twisted my arms behind my back, as if I were a criminal.

Another man, dressed in a suit, came in and my captors released the pressure on my head.

'So this is the guy, is it?' he said. 'It's taken me fucking for ever to track you down!'

He turned to Gold Teeth: 'Wasn't the lead in that 1950s film *Tibetan Serfs* called Champa?'

Gold Teeth shrugged and the Suit answered himself: 'It definitely was.'

I stood naked, jammed between the pair of them. The Suit glanced at my crotch: 'Well, that's not much to get excited about! You're hardly a stud. And you really thought you could get away with the whole lot, including the fancy Range Rover?' He looked around the room.

'Where's your girlfriend?'

I didn't answer, there was no point. Shell's bra, knickers, top and trousers were all on the floor. They looked at the toilet door.

'Come out, girlie!' said Suit. 'Come and take a little walk with us.' Then he said: 'If you don't come out, we're coming in.'

'I'm coming out,' said Shell.

The toilet door opened and Shell came out, dressed only in an overcoat with nothing underneath. They all leered at her.

'Uncle An!' Shell greeted the Suit coldly.

The Suit looked taken aback. 'Shell?'

'Did my mum tell you to come?'

The Suit pulled himself together. 'So this is all family business, is it? What an idiot! I should have known . . .

'You've got a fucking cheek, haven't you?' This was addressed to me. Then he went on: 'I'm not getting mixed up in family business. We're off. Shell, you sort it out with your mum.'

'No,' said Shell. 'You go and talk to her. You came here because she told you to.'

'All right, all right,' the Suit said unwillingly. 'I'll talk to her if you won't. Come and see me when you've got time, Shell. I'll take you out for a meal.'

'No, thank you, Uncle,' said Shell, her voice hard as flint.

The Suit rubbed his nose helplessly and left. The rest of them followed behind looking disappointed.

When they shut the door, Shell asked me: 'You didn't tell my mum we were together?'

My hand pressed to my ribs, I said: 'I didn't say it was you.'

'What were you thinking of? If you didn't tell her it was me, she was never going to let you go, was she?'

7

Overnight, the news about Shell and me had got out, and the next morning a friend of Shell's called. Shell looked anxious and said to hang on, she was going outside. She went out and shut the door so I couldn't hear what she was saying.

My ribs still hurt. What was the point in having all those sinews and flesh if a single punch was that painful? Gold Teeth had been so quick with his fists. How could I have got one back at him? I was still furious at being made to stand there without a stitch of clothing on like a criminal. Furious at myself too, for being scared and not daring to resist. I could have given the Suit a savage kick when he came up close, then lashed out left and right and felled the other two, but for the life of me I couldn't work out how I could have dealt with Gold Teeth too. I'd stood there like an idiot, not daring to move, waiting on Shell to come out and get me off the hook.

Who was 'Uncle An'? And how did they know I was here?

'Who's Uncle An?' I asked.

'A friend of my mum's,' said Shell, not looking at me.

'What does he do?'

'How do I know? Runs a security firm or something. He used to be in the police. Nothing to do with me.'

'How did they know I was here?'

She shrugged but obviously didn't want to talk.

Shell was really pissed off. I was pissed off too but who could I take it out on? I was the one who'd been hit, I was the one who'd been humiliated, and I wasn't getting any sympathy; in fact, she was picking a fight with me for not having told her mum I was with her. It's true, I hadn't said. Did she think I was going to write in a text: 'I've fallen in love with your daughter'?

Shell said nothing more, and went back to sleep. Fine by me. The pain in my ribs kept me awake, and I don't think Shell slept well either. By getting off with me she'd taken her mum's boyfriend, so it wasn't surprising she was feeling bad.

When I woke up in the morning, Shell was already browsing on her laptop.

All morning, she was either on the laptop or on the phone. I went out for a stroll. When I got back, I said: 'Li says it's lunch time.' Shell just shook her head – she didn't want anything to eat.

At one point, Shell finished a phone call and came back inside to say: 'Some friends of mine have invited us for a meal this evening, to welcome you to Beijing.'

That cheered me up a lot.

'They'd like to know what you want to eat.'

'Peking duck,' I said, without a moment's hesitation.

8

Shell needed to go into Beijing for work and I wanted to go and buy some clothes for the dinner tonight with her friends. It was warm, and I only had the Harley leather jacket, too hot in this weather. My jeans smelled of dogs. My jeans had never been washed, jeans are cowboy gear after all, but that didn't mean they had to stink of dogs.

Shell dropped me off at the Yashow clothing market in Chaoyang district and said she'd be back in three hours to pick me up, she had to do a few things nearby. I went in. A load of foreigners were standing around haggling. I loathed bargaining and, anyway, everything looked like fake designer gear and Plum always said she didn't want me buying fake labels. Why had Shell brought me to a market like this? I wandered aimlessly around. Then, on one stall, I suddenly saw the exact same leather jacket as the one I was wearing.

I walked straight out of the market. Surely Plum hadn't come to a place like this and fobbed me off with a fake Harley jacket?

I wandered along and found myself in a nearby shopping centre. There was a big two-storey Apple store and several clothing and food stores. The shop signs weren't in Chinese but I recognized them anyway. Big stores like these wouldn't be selling fake labels. I went into the one that had a C and a K in the name and bought a pair of jeans, a T-shirt and a black blazer, paying with my own bank card. Then I went into a shoe shop and bought a pair of trainers with a leopard logo on. I'd seen the logo in magazine adverts.

There was a small plaza in the centre, where I did a bit of people-watching. I'd changed into my new clothes and was carrying the old ones, checking my iPhone from time to time. I reckon I could pass for a Beijinger now; in fact, I was better-looking. True, I was darker-skinned but that was just suntan.

I suppose I ought to have been more modest – after all, I was what they called an 'outlander', I should have looked up to these city folk. But honestly I couldn't see any difference between them and me. I strolled along until I got to a Kentucky Fried Chicken. In front, a couple of Tibetan men and an older woman, all from the Ngawa prefecture in Kham, had set up a stall. They were selling cheap trinkets, not a patch on the luxury goods Plum sold. They were very friendly; they offered me a knock-down price because I was a compatriot. I asked what kind of things Beijing girls liked and they all talked at once. One of them showed me a turquoise brooch. It looked quite decent and I bought it, at their compatriot discount.

Shell came and picked me up, and I threw my bag of purchases on the back seat. 'What did you buy?' she asked. 'Not much,' I said, 'just one of each. The bag's got my old things in.' I showed off what I was wearing. 'Nice, eh?'

Shell gave a slight nod, then said: 'How much?'

'Less than 5,000 the lot,' I said. Her eyes widened slightly but she said nothing.

I got out the turquoise brooch. 'This is a present for you.' I found Shell's expression hard to read, she seemed both embarrassed and touched. 'I'll pin it on you,' I offered, but she wanted to do it herself. She took it and stuck it on her collar without looking at it.

9

That evening, we ate in an old Beijing restaurant in the Chaoyang area, and her friends were all very nice to me except for Wang

Dajun's wife. We had just begun on the cold starters when she butted in with: 'Shell, I asked the manager at Makye Ame Tibetan Restaurant and he's happy for Champa to go and talk to him about a job.'

Shell glanced at me. I was taken aback. 'I'm not going to skivvy for a Tibetan boss here,' I said. What a climb-down that would be.

'Would you be interested in working in the Companion Animal shop, Champa?' said Mrs Qing. 'You don't have to buy and sell animals.' Half joking, I said: 'Haven't I done enough voluntary work? I don't want to specialize in pet care. I reckon working in a pet shop is women's work.'

Wang Dajun's wife said icily: 'You don't have any qualifications. It's not easy for outlanders to get work in Beijing.' No one spoke.

'What kind of work do you want to do?' Another question from Wang's wife.

Bloody hell! When had I ever asked her to get me a job? What was she in such a rush for? I'd only been here a few days, and I hadn't had enough fun yet.

'I want to run my own nightclub,' I said. 'I read an article in a fashion magazine about a Mongolian guy who came to Beijing and worked as a security guard at a nightclub. Then someone gave him the money to set up a nightclub of his own. Just the refurbishment cost 37 million *yuan*!'

Still no one said anything. This time, I thought, I've really shut them up. Then I added: 'Don't worry. That's just my dream. My friend Nyima says that dreams are so beautiful why bother making them come true?'

Wang Dajun roared with laughter, and the others smiled too, except Wang's wife, who was completely humourless and sat there stony-faced. Shell didn't smile either but she wasn't stony-faced, probably just thinking about something else.

After that, everyone around the table went on talking and laughing, except Wang's wife and Shell. They asked me what there was to see in Tibet. I told them all about the various places tourists went to, and they seemed to think my opinions were worth listening to.

I felt that my Chinese had improved by leaps and bounds since my arrival in Beijing.

The Peking duck was delicious. Too bad no one was drinking. Since I was their guest, I couldn't very well order red wine and drink it on my own.

'Champa, why don't we get a taxi and go to the Tibetan Bar outside the west gate of Nationalities University? Lots of the Tibetan students go there,' suggested Dan Dan, who had finished eating first. Wang's wife said grimly: 'He's not a university student.' Then Shell chipped in: 'No, you all go, I have to drive, and besides, Champa's tired.'

As we drove home, I asked Shell: 'Why did you say I was tired? I'm not tired.'

'But didn't you say you wanted to stay away from Tibetans?'

'No, I said I didn't want to skivvy for a Tibetan boss,' I said.

Shell said nothing.

I thought: Don't you go putting words in my mouth. It was you who asked those women to get me a job, wasn't it? But I held off saying anything out loud.

10

Shell said that starting from the next day, she'd have to stay in her town flat for about a week because she was the stage designer for a play being put on in some small theatre or other. She needed to be there, she couldn't let them down. They'd be rehearsing every day until late in the evening, so she wouldn't be able to come back to be with me.

'What play is it?' I asked.

She showed me the playbill. 'Beijing's *Waiting for Godot*', it was called. I'd never heard of it. The Chinese play that we Tibetans most enjoyed was the adventure classic *Journey to the West*.

I said I could go to the theatre every day. I mean, I liked watching actors at live performances. I often used to go to the Nangma dance clubs in Lhasa. Then we could go back to her place for the night. I'd had enough of the kennels, I'd rather be in her flat in town so I could go and look around.

She was silent, but I knew she was building up to tell me something.

She sounded as if she'd rehearsed it in advance. 'There's someone else in my town flat. What I'm trying to say is, I live with someone. Actually, he keeps me. I couldn't support myself on the little I earn from a few design jobs, let alone these dogs. I haven't told him about us yet, so I've got to go back there and tell him. I'll do it as soon as I can, and I'll finish with him. I promise you that.'

So she had someone else. I wasn't too happy about that but Shell had said she'd dump him, so what could I say?

'You stay here a few days. I told Yang and the other girls that you would and they're fine about it,' Shell said. 'When it gets busy here, the volunteers stay overnight anyway. So you can stay too. When I've finished this job, I'll look for a place for us to live.'

But I hadn't come to Beijing to live in a dog kennel. It was way more scruffy than anywhere I'd lived in Lhasa. 'Tell him tomorrow and move out, and we'll go and find a hotel,' I said.

She shook her head. 'There's no way I can tell him for the next few days. It'll have to wait till the play's over. He put a lot of money into this production and it means a lot to us. I can't risk spoiling things for the others because of my private life. Trust me. Just wait a few more days.'

I really didn't like the idea of Shell going back to some other man's flat. 'But so many people know, if you don't tell him, someone else will,' I said unhappily.

Shell said nothing for a moment. Then: 'I've asked people to keep quiet, and they move in different circles anyway. I hope no one's going to put their foot in it and mess things up.' She looked away from me, out of the car window: 'I've already messed things up, haven't I?'

11

Another day dawned in the kennels. I carried on shovelling dog shit.

In the afternoon I drove to the pet clinic to fetch the dogs that had been receiving treatment. They were all much better and greeted me like an old friend, leaping up and licking me all over. Good thing I was wearing those old trousers, my 'dog uniform'.

All the volunteers talked about all day was dogs, or cats. There'd been quite a few incidents, all over China, where volunteers had intercepted lorry-loads of dogs or cats being taken to the butcher. One of the lorries, in Chongqing, turned out to contain over a thousand dogs, though they only had the paperwork for five hundred. The other five hundred had been stuffed in illegally. In the town of Qinhuangdao, in Hebei province, the volunteers intercepted three dog traders' lorries and got beaten up. When the police turned up, they dispersed the volunteers and let the traders go. And in Tianjin, a lorry with seven hundred cats on board was stopped. It was on its way to Guangdong in the south, where they still eat cats.

The volunteers from the dogs home were exhausted by the latest incident. It was too much responsibility, and all the dogs or cats had to be cared for once they'd taken them in. They couldn't go on like this. They were paying over money to the dog-meat men who then paid dog thieves to go and steal more dogs. But what else could they do? Was there any prospect that the government would legislate to stop the trade? As for lorries in transit, some volunteers thought they shouldn't meddle with them, but others thought that if you came across one, you should surely try and save some of the animals. You had to judge each case on its own merits.

I wasn't obsessed with animals, and I didn't care for the dogs and cats the way they did, but I could understand their pain. I chatted with everyone and they were very friendly.

But I was not happy. I'd been in China for days and every day the weather was grey and overcast. I felt like I was in a dream, walking and walking but always stuck in the same place.

I decided there was no damned way I was going to stay around tomorrow. I'd get away before the volunteers came, and go for a drive around Beijing to orientate myself. I couldn't even tell which was north at the moment, stuck here in this dog kennel, because it was all flat round about, there were no landmarks. I wanted to go and see the sights. Since Shell couldn't come with me, I'd take myself out and have some fun.

I went online and looked at car sales websites. Beijing had its annual New Car Exhibition and there would be more than a thousand models on show. There were 120 new models making their world debut, alone. Cool. I'd go. Tomorrow I'd drive myself to the Beijing Car Show in the Range Rover Aurora, dressed in my new clothes. Let me by, guys and girls! Hey, girlie, you know what kind of car this is? It's a Range Rover Aurora! Pretty nice, eh? You just tell me if there's anything nicer in the show!

This was the reason why I'd come to Beijing. To broaden my horizons. That was what my granddad used to say in his broken Chinese: 'Go to Beijing to broaden your horizons.'

I felt better after that.

That evening, I got thinking. Shell was right. Now that Plum knew I was with her daughter, she wouldn't come looking for me. Lucky for me that their relationship was so screwed up – and that meant she'd been happy to spring the trap and let me out. Hah! Shell was the one person that Plum didn't dare upset. Shell was her *karma* from a past life. Just like A-Lan said, Plum hated people leaving her. Shell was right – it was because I was with her and not some other girl that Plum had let me off the hook so easily.

Gold Teeth had landed a punch in my ribs. His boss, Shell's 'Uncle An', had acted as if I was a conman, a gigolo and a car thief. If they had taken me away, who knows how bad things would have been for me?

The thought was scarcely out of my head when Gold Teeth's car drove in fast through the compound gates. I bellowed for the caretaker: 'Li!'

Gold Teeth got out of the car with another man. Again, he seemed delighted to see me and bared his teeth in a huge grin. He reached out his left hand, this time as if he wanted something off me. Mr and Mrs Li stood in the doorway watching. I raised both fists to protect my rib cage. My mobile rang and Gold Teeth gestured to me to answer it. I kept my guard up and ignored him. 'Answer the phone!' he commanded.

I could see it was Shell calling. She'd come to my aid. 'Shell . . .' I said into the phone, but she got in first. 'Champa, listen to me. I've just had a call from Uncle An. He says Mum wants everything back, that is, everything you brought with you. I told Uncle An you'd give back the Range Rover but the rest, forget it. Give the car back but hang on to the iPad and the iPhone and stuff. I've got Uncle An to agree to that. In a bit, his men'll turn up and collect the car. Are you listening, Champa?'

'They're already here,' I said.

'Then give them the car, OK? Then they'll leave you alone. Champa?'

'OK.'

'I'll hang up now. Keep your phone on.'

'Uh-huh.'

Gold Teeth held out his left hand once more. I asked him the question which had been on my mind. 'How did you know I was here yesterday?' He didn't answer, just bared his teeth and jerked his outstretched hand expectantly. There was nothing for it. I chucked the car keys over, and he caught them easily, then flipped them over to the man next to him.

Before he got into the car, he flourished his mobile above his head and tossed and caught it a couple of times, making sure I saw what he was doing.

The mobile? Was that how they found me? The mobile signal?

12

I wandered along the road in a daze. After a few hundred metres, I passed a housing estate and saw the supermarket was still open. I'd go and buy some drink, it didn't matter what drink, just so long as it was alcoholic. Everyone knew that we Tibetans liked our drink, so why shouldn't I? The supermarket was super-small but it had a few kinds of wine and a bottle opener. I chose the cheapest dry Chinese red, only twenty *yuan* a bottle. Since I was aiming to get drunk, there was no point in getting anything more expensive. I cleaned the shop out of its stock – nine bottles – bought a bottle opener and carried everything back to my dog kennel.

They'd taken my car and I was bereft. All these years, how long was it since I'd been without a car? I'd lived with my car, it was part of me. I could live in a dog kennel but I couldn't live without a car. I'd forgotten what it was like to be without wheels. I couldn't go anywhere, couldn't do anything . . . I was desolate and there was no light at the end of the tunnel.

Plum had told me the Range Rover was mine. 'Nice car?' she'd said. 'Very,' I'd answered. 'It's yours. You and me are going back to Lhasa in it. You can drive. Like it?' That was how our conversation had gone.

I loved it so much I'd forgotten I was only the driver.

It wasn't mine and I'd just given it back.

When Li came to wake me up the next morning, he said the room stank of drink. That afternoon, I asked Yang: 'A third-hand Xiali can't cost much more than a few thousand *yuan* in Beijing, can it?'

'It's a bit more complicated than that,' she told me. 'There's a new city regulation – you have to apply for a number plate and it's a lucky dip. Shell was lucky, right after she'd passed her test, one of the volunteers let her have a Skoda dirt cheap and she got her number plate just before the new regulations came into effect.'

I realized that, however I looked at it, there was no way I could afford a car and a number plate in Beijing. I finally faced the ugly truth that I'd never have my own car in this city.

Every time I shovelled a dog turd, I said to myself: You're just a dog turd, you've got the luck of a turd. With these new regulations, you can't even drive an old car. And you still think Beijing welcomes you? You're a dog turd, with the luck of a turd.

Old Li got out a bus map and tried to show me the bus routes. Probably because for the last day or two I'd talked of nothing but this car show, he was determined to tell me how to get there by bus. I was only half listening. I didn't want to appear ungrateful but I really didn't want to go any more. I would have enjoyed driving there in the Range Rover. Now I didn't have a car, going to look at other people's would just be rubbing salt in the wound. Besides, what was the point, if I couldn't afford one and had no chance of getting a licence plate either?

After dinner, I started drinking again. I drank myself into a stupor, dozed a bit, and was then woken up by the phone. It was Shell.

'It's me, Champa. We've just finished the first performance. It went really well.'

I couldn't seem to get my tongue around the words. 'Dog turd, Shell, luck of a dog turd.'

'Are you OK, Champa?'

'I'm OK, bottle only twenty *yuan*. Shell, you said I can't buy a car, I wanna scooter, OK?'

'Champa, you're pissed! I'm going to ask Li to go and see to you.'

'Gotta stay on till Dabeiyao, Beijing, China, then change buses . . . thass what he said . . .'

13

I don't know if Li came over or not. I woke up at midday. Shell was back. Her Skoda was packed full of suitcases and other stuff. She was moving in. The Lis and I helped her carry everything from the car and, by the time we'd finished, there wasn't room to swing a cat. No one asked why she'd brought all her stuff with her, until finally I asked.

''Cos I finished with him.'

'Really?' I was excited. 'Didn't you say you had to wait until the play had finished its run?'

'Well, after I phoned you last night, I started to think. I could handle one more night there but this morning I realized that was it, so I told him.'

She touched the side of her face with a wry smile.

'Did he hit you?' I asked. She nodded.

'Bastard! I'll get him.'

She shook her head. 'I got one back at him, knocked his nose sideways, he had to go to the hospital. So we're quits. I don't know why he hit me. He's got a husband.'

Now I was really confused. He's got a husband? I didn't pick her up on it though, just said: 'So . . . are you going to the theatre later?'

'No, I don't feel like it. I don't want to see her.'

'But shouldn't you go? You're the stage designer, what will they do without you?'

'There's an assistant. They've had the first performance, we've done everything we had to do, they don't need me any more.'

'I need you,' I said. 'I really need you.'

Shell smiled but the smile turned into a grimace of pain. I went and put my arms around her: 'I need you so much!' I gripped her small buttocks hard and pressed myself against her, but she suddenly went, 'No,' and pushed me off. 'I've come on,' she said. Then: 'I'll bring you off.'

She jammed the chair against the door. I just stood there, and she unzipped my jeans and pulled them down. Then she pushed me over to the bed and jerked me off. I badly wanted her to take me in her mouth but she just used her thumb and two fingers, ever so lightly, and I didn't have the heart to ask her to.

14

The next morning, Shell asked me to drive her into town. She seemed even less keen on our dog kennel than I was.

We went to an area called Shuangjing and found an estate agent. We told her we wanted to rent a flat and we were willing to pay 3,000 *yuan* a month for a place with at least two bedrooms and a living room. She said that one exactly like that for about that price was ready to view, and took us there straight away. She said the owner had been allocated it by her work unit, and it sounded very nice. A middle-aged woman opened the door to us and immediately gave me a strange look. It was as if she'd never seen anyone who looked Tibetan before. 'Have you got a work permit for Beijing?' she asked. 'We're from Beijing,' protested Shell. The woman said nothing, just stared poker-faced at me. Shell seemed to like the flat and whispered to me that it was OK. Actually, I didn't think much of it. To me, it was shabby and cramped. The living room was just a corridor and the kitchen and bathroom needed decorating. But I'd let Shell decide.

'Have you got your marriage certificate?' The woman was speaking again.

'Auntie,' Shell replied sweetly, 'we're renting the flat so we can get married.'

But the woman latched on to this. 'Oh, no,' she said firmly. 'In that case, I can't rent it to you.'

The estate agent was on our side: 'Auntie, they'll be married soon, and then it'll be all right.'

But the woman refused to budge. Shell gave up and we left.

I tried to comfort Shell: 'I didn't like it much. The kitchen was too small. I like big kitchens. And, I don't know if you saw, but the bathroom had no window. I don't like bathrooms without windows.'

There was a lot of discussion between Shell and the estate agent and, when we went to view another flat, they made me wait outside while they went in.

I wasn't too happy about that but I wasn't prepared to argue in front of a stranger.

We looked at two but Shell didn't like either. She said they were no bigger than the first and a lot more expensive. I pulled a long face. The estate agent suggested we try around the Tongzhou or Wangjing areas, but Shell insisted she wanted somewhere on the east side of town.

She looked despondent. 'Rents have really gone up,' she said. 'Let's not see any more today.'

I tried to cheer her up by teasing her when we passed a Pizza Hut. 'Look, there's your favourite food!'

Shell smiled and said: 'Don't be cheeky.'

We had bowls of sour and hot noodles for dinner and I said: 'Shell, let's not worry too much about money. If we see something we like, let's go for it, even if it does cost a bit more. I can pay with my card.'

'My mum's probably already cancelled your credit card.'

'No, I mean my own bank card. I've saved money from my wages, it's mine.'

'How much have you got?'

'More than 10,000 *yuan*.'

Shell looked at me: 'Champa, in Beijing, that's nothing. You keep it. And don't spend it all at once, eh?'

In the afternoon, we were back at the kennels. The volunteers were all talking about a picture A-Shan had put up on her twitter account, of a middle-aged man who was known to catch stray dogs for the pot, in Beijing's back alleys. A-Shan had hunted him down, sneaked a picture of him and posted it online.

Dan Dan introduced her new boyfriend to us. He was a very tall, thin man with a neat, little goatee beard that made him look like an actor in a Japanese TV drama. I kept wondering why had he left those hairs on his chin. Goatee looked at the banner over the entrance and said gravely to Shell: 'That's mind-blowing, "Let living creatures stray no longer". That's me, a creature that strays, like a bird with no legs, which just has to keep flying on and on, and sleeps in the wind.'

I nearly laughed out loud.

Goatee looked at Shell: 'Have you heard that before?'

'Of course I have,' retorted Shell. 'It was Leslie Cheung Kwok-wing.'

'And the film?' he pressed her.

'*Days of Being Wild.*'

Goatee got quite emotional. 'Oh yes indeed! Wong Kar-wai's *Days of Being Wild* is one of my ten best films, because that's what I am, a legless bird!'

I thought Shell would change the subject, but she came back with: 'And what are the other nine?' And they reeled off the names of a load of arty films that no one had ever heard of. I was getting bored, but Dan Dan was standing there hanging on their every word. It was pretty obvious to me that Goatee was just trying to get off with Shell.

I went and talked to the other girls. They showed me all the abusive tweets about the dog-eating man. They seemed to think the way to change people's eating and drinking habits was abusing someone online.

'Does anyone here want a driver, or do you know anyone who does?' I asked. But it turned out that they either used public transport or had cheap cars and couldn't afford drivers. 'How about bodyguards then?' I said jokingly, flexing my biceps at them. 'Wouldn't you like me as your private bodyguard? Ten per cent discount for pretty girls!' They all thought I was very funny and I cheered up a bit.

'Why did you go around offering yourself to the girls as their driver or bodyguard?' Shell asked that evening, sounding annoyed.

'I need work. I can't stick around here all day.'

'So now you think you need to get a job, do you?' she said, still staring at her computer screen.

I didn't rise to the bait, just said: 'Didn't you say that your uncle An ran a security company? A few years ago, maybe a hundred young Tibetan men were recruited as guards by a Beijing company. The regional government and the Lhasa police thought this was a great idea, and it was all on the TV. I could be any kind of a guard . . . nightclub bouncer, shop security, residential compound guard, filmstar's personal bodyguard, you name it . . .'

Shell ignored me.

'Will you talk to him, Shell?' I asked.

'Shouldn't you be a bit more ambitious than that?' she snapped.

She was on her laptop all evening and ignored me completely. I didn't know if she was working or just messaging her friends. I played Angry Birds and drank my wine. I was annoyed that she'd been so abrupt with me and avoided speaking to her. I looked around the room, it was such a mess, it really was no better than a dog kennel. Shell never picked up after herself, the suitcases were open and things were left lying all over the place, panties, bras, socks, all jumbled up. She hadn't worn the turquoise brooch I'd bought her, or put it away either, it was lying on the floor too. When we intercepted the lorry that day, she'd acted like a real leader, great at organizing other people, just like her mum. But here at home, she couldn't even keep her things under control. Stuff was strewn around as if she was a street vendor. The thing that most bothered me was her period. She said she'd come on but she wasn't drinking much water and I hadn't seen her going to the bathroom much during the day. I really didn't understand these girls.

The next day, Shell said she'd go and look at flats. 'Everyone's been asking me where I live now,' she said, looking wretched, 'and I'm too embarrassed to tell them.' She told me not to go with her, as she had other stuff to do in town too. Then she drove off.

15

There were always new people turning up at the kennels. It was the weekend, and two girls came along. They were not particularly pretty, but they were certainly very young – still at university. They were doing foreign languages and called themselves weird foreign names, Sarah and Liza. I called them Salad and Ricer, to tease them. What I was really interested in was Ricer's chocolate brown Mini Cooper, so I chatted them up and asked if I could have a go at driving it. They were cool, and said of course I could.

Just then, Yang came over. A-Shan had called to say that someone had messaged her about an old woman in a back alley in the Dongcheng district who had just died, leaving two cats with no one to feed them. A-Shan was out of town on business, could one of us go and check it out? Salad and Ricer jumped at the chance. Yang relayed the message and asked for the exact address.

It didn't seem like I was invited, but then Salad said: 'Champa, you come too, and I'll sit in the back.' Salad was tiny, so she could just about squeeze in. She said to me quietly, while Ricer was still talking to Yang: 'Ricer's only just passed her test.'

I was only too happy to take a tour around Beijing's back alleys with two young girls in such a cool car. It was a good thing I was driving too, as the lanes were hard to manoeuvre. We drove round and round before we finally found the alley. It was only twenty or thirty metres long and so narrow that, once we were in, it was going to be hard to get out, even in this little car. The place had to be somewhere behind one of those walls, so I let Salad and Ricer out and went off to find somewhere to park.

It was a good thing it was a Mini. I drove up and down a couple of lanes and found a small parking space. But any driver less skilled than me wouldn't have been able to get into it.

I went back to the alley. The houses were all derelict, with no one living in them and probably due for demolition. Behind a crumbling old wall I heard a man's voice on the other side: 'Which of you is A-Shan?'

Inside, half a dozen burly men were standing round the girls. I heard Ricer say calmly: 'Neither of us.'

'So what are you doing here then?'

'We've come to rescue the cats,' said Salad.

'So it was A-Shan who sent you!' said one of the men triumphantly and, turning to his mates, said: 'You see. They took the bait.'

I could see the speaker now. It was the man A-Shan had hunted down and posted online, the dog-eater. One of the other men was gloating. 'So you think it's only bitches like you who can play at tweeting.'

Ricer was getting upset. 'It wasn't us who tweeted. We don't know A-Shan. We're just student volunteers.'

Dog-eater said: 'You stupid little bitch. I loathe volunteers. What do they think they're doing, hunting down a respectable man like me?'

'What do you want?' asked Ricer.

'Want?' said Dog-eater. 'Well, you could start by making it up to me.'

Salad burst into tears at that. There was nothing for it – I marched boldly into the yard: 'Good afternoon, gentlemen.'

They looked scared, and backed off. 'I'm sorry to bother you,' I said. 'I'll take the girls away. Excuse me, sir.'

'It's only him, there's no one else,' one said, realizing I was alone, and they all blocked me in. Another had a cosh in his hand. 'He's not from Beijing, is he?' he said. They seemed to be goading each other on. 'Excuse me,' I tried again. 'This really has nothing to do with them.'

'So it's to do with you?' said Cosh.

'No, not me either,' I said.

'Well, if it's nothing to do with you, then get out of here,' said Dog-eater. 'I want a chat with these girlies.' And he closed in on Ricer.

I could see he was determined to take advantage of her and I couldn't let that happen. I stepped forward: 'I'd advise you to go and find A-Shan. She's the one who fitted you up.'

'You looking for trouble, or something?' Dog-eater turned on me, and they all jeered.

'We're all grown men here. Leave these girls alone. You're scaring them.'

'This lad's really looking for trouble,' said Dog-eater.

I could see there was going to be a fight. Too bad, there was no way I could deal with so many single-handed. Salad had me by the hand and was pulling me away. She was pulling me off balance and I wished she'd stop tugging.

Ricer began to plead with them. 'Please accept my apologies, I'm so sorry. We're just immature young girls. Please, sirs, forgive us.'

'Cut the crap,' said one of the men.

'You could start by making it up to me,' said Dog-eater again.

'How do you mean, "making it up to you"?' said Ricer, trembling.

The men weren't giving up now that the girls were visibly nervous. A sudden intuition made me take out my mobile. I took a picture of the thugs and quickly pressed a few numbers.

'He's taken a picture!' said one. 'Get his phone.'

'I've already sent it,' I lied. 'It was a good picture, you're all in it, nice and clear. You won't get away with this.' That cooled them down a bit.

Cosh was still holding his weapon and I took another shot of him: 'Gotcha. That's one of the cosh too. It's all evidence. Thugs have gotta be stopped.' That upset them, and they began muttering amongst themselves.

'So are you going to behave yourselves or not?' I persisted.

Dog-eater suddenly acted as if nothing had happened. 'Hey, brother, we haven't done anything. We're just ordinary blokes, having a harmless joke.'

'That's right,' added one. 'Just a harmless joke.' And another: 'We were just out for a stroll. What's wrong with a bunch of ordinary blokes out for a stroll?'

'Nothing at all,' I said. 'You go for your stroll. We'll clear off.' Salad and Ricer were trembling. Making a show of being cool as a cucumber, I took each of them by the arm and we left the court-yard. I wished I had eyes in the back of my head so I could see if they were going to jump us. But they didn't.

16

'Violence doesn't solve anything!' said Shell. That was the first clue that everyone else had a completely different take on what had happened. I didn't expect a hero's welcome, but I did think they might have given me credit for being brave and smart.

Salad and Ricer had been very quiet in the car. I don't know whether they were scared, or whether they didn't like having fallen into a trap. I knew what that felt like. Then they each began sending texts. Back at the kennels, I told them to report what had happened to Yang. It was better for these girls to explain it in their own words. I went off to have a snooze.

When I woke up in the evening, I discovered everyone had gone without saying goodbye. Old Li told me that Yang had taken everyone off for a meeting with Wang Dajun and his group.

'Did you nearly get into a fight?' asked the old man.

'Nearly,' I said.

Li went off home then. I was pissed off the others had had a meeting and hadn't called me in, as the person most involved.

Shell was very late back. She got straight on to her computer and hardly said anything to me. I couldn't help asking: 'How are Salad and Ricer?'

Shell was still looking at her screen. 'They've gone back to their campus.'

'Were they scared?' I asked.

'They're OK,' she said. Then she added: 'They're Beijing girls.'

What did the fact they were Beijing girls have to do with anything? I said: 'Those thugs certainly scared the hell out of them today.'

'You misunderstood,' said Shell, not looking at me.

I'd misunderstood? 'Things were pretty hairy. It was a good thing I was there,' I protested.

'These blokes from Beijing back alleys, however thuggish they are, would never get up to any mischief with female students. That's what you misunderstood.'

'If I hadn't got involved, those thugs might have done anything. They weren't ordinary Beijing blokes.'

Finally, she looked up at me. 'You thought things were getting hairy, so they did. You're too hasty and too suspicious, that's what really worries me about you. You overreacted, and let it get out of hand.' Shell turned back to her laptop. Her parting shot was: 'Violence doesn't solve anything.'

This was the last thing I expected. Me violent? Knocking someone's nose sideways, now that was violent. I asked, puzzled: 'Is that what you all really think about me?'

'It's all "me, me, me" with you!' Shell snapped. 'We never talked about you. What we talked about was how important it is that animal protection volunteers should never be involved in violence. If that happens, the media will never support us again. We were also talking about how to verify reports we receive about strays, to put a stop to more mischief like this.'

Mischief! I remembered how, as soon as Dog-eater heard me take a photo, he completely changed his tune to 'we were only having a harmless joke' and backed off. And now everyone else was treating it as a harmless joke too.

I turned on Shell and shouted: 'OK, next time you girls fall into a trap like that, don't expect me to come and rescue you!'

As I went out, I heard Shell mutter: 'You're nuts!'

17

The next afternoon, we went to the Companion Animals Adoption Day, which was being held on a bit of empty space outside a computer mall not far from Chaoyang Gate. Shell, of course, was going to help and I'd told Melon-head I'd go too.

It was a brilliantly sunny day. It was the first time I'd seen the sun in Beijing. There was a strange smell in the air. I asked Shell what it was, and she said it was locust tree blossom. It smells like semen, I said. Shell said nothing. Beijing's awash with the smell of men's sperm and people just call it blossom, I thought to myself.

Adoption Day events were doing better and better apparently. They attracted lots of people, especially young people who thought it would be fun to adopt a cat or dog. The volunteers took their work seriously. Interested adopters first had to register, then the next day a volunteer would do a home visit to vet the adopter, see whether they could afford it and whether they were mentally stable. After an adoption, a volunteer would make another visit to make sure the pet was being properly cared for. These girls had such a sense of responsibility towards the animals, even I found it quite moving.

Melon-head gave me some pain-killing ointment and went off to take care of something. The day before, at the kennels, I'd told him my rib cage hurt and he said he'd bring me some.

I met plenty of volunteers I knew today. Apart from Wang Dajun's wife, the rest were all very friendly. Wang himself was as enthusiastic as usual but didn't stop to talk to me. In fact, no one stopped to ask me what happened yesterday.

Dan Dan's boyfriend with the Japanese-style goatee had come and was deep in conversation with Shell. That really pissed me off. Shell hardly ever had a proper conversation with me, I mean the kind where you say something and I say something back. But that was what she was doing with Goatee. I could see them engrossed. And I couldn't do it with Shell. Not even a little bit.

I wandered away from the Adoption Fair and went into the computer mall. There were two girls in pussy-high mini-skirts looking at the mobiles, and I stood some distance away staring at them and their long legs. But when they left, I went back to the fair.

There was a small stage, and a singer was performing. The crowds kept turning up. I looked everywhere for Shell and finally saw her, standing in a corner with her back to me, with a woman who looked a little older. They were tête-à-tête, the older woman talking and Shell listening intently. The woman had a sticking plaster on her nose. Their little fingers were intertwined.

I went to the Walmart above the car park on the opposite side of the road. There was a deal on bottles of imported red wine and I bought a dozen. Then I saw some half-bottles with screw caps and added two more. I went and dumped them in the boot of Shell's car, sat in the driver's seat and drank the two half-bottles.

Shell called and I told her I was in the car. She came and got in, then immediately pulled a face: 'Drinking in the daytime?'

'Just half-bottles,' I said. 'Where are we going now?'

'Move over, I'll drive.'

'No, let me,' I said. 'I'm not drunk.'

Shell was angry. 'This is Beijing, not Lhasa. You stick to the law here, OK?'

18

Back at the kennels, I carried on drowning my sorrows. Somehow I found myself blurting out: 'And what were you chatting on about to that woman with the sticking plaster on her nose?'

That got Shell's attention. She was quite still for a moment, then she slowly turned away from the computer and looked at me. 'She said she's got a bed-sit I can move into.'

'A bed-sit? How big is it?'

'Thirty square metres,' Shell said, reluctantly.

That sure as hell was small. 'When can we move in?' I asked.

There was that inscrutable expression on her face again. This time, it seemed like embarrassment. She turned back to the computer and said, without looking at me: 'It's too small.'

She said nothing more. The brooch I'd given her was still lying there in a corner, where it had been for days. Knickers and bras littered the floor. She didn't seem to have washed any of her knickers or socks either. I didn't wash my jeans, but I washed and dried my T-shirts and underwear each time I wore them, then folded them neatly and put them away. Shell didn't wash or fold or put away anything, just left it lying around. She spent all night on the computer, didn't drink any water or go to the bathroom. Was she constipated? Hadn't she told me she had her period? Well, I hadn't seen any blood or any sanitary towels. Fuck it, didn't she change her sanitary pads either?

I got though two bottles of wine. I was pissed but the wine hadn't done anything for my mood. Shell was lying face-down on the bed with just her knickers on, her eyes half closed. Her jeans were lying in a heap on the floor. I don't believe you've got your period, I thought. It was time for a 'spurt of the moment'.

I turned her over and got on top of her. She struggled. 'What do you think you're doing?' I pulled her knickers down and pushed her legs apart. I stuck my middle finger up her cunt, then pulled it out and looked at it. No blood. I pushed my cock into her. She was going to scream but I kept my hand clamped over her mouth and thrust in and out. She just lay there silent until I came. My semen smelled really strong, just like the locust tree blossom in the streets.

19

Afterwards, Shell went into the toilet and shut the door. At first there was no sound, then I seemed to hear her crying. I didn't feel so drunk any more. I felt bad that I'd been rough with her and waited for her to come out of the toilet so I could say sorry. But the wine put me to sleep and I didn't wake up till morning.

When I opened my eyes, Shell was sitting on a chair bent forward with both hands clasping her belly. She was wearing a formal pencil skirt.

'Does it still hurt? Do you want to go to the hospital?' I asked.

Shell shook her head. 'It's just cramps. My period's coming.'

She seemed exhausted, but she sat up and addressed me, as if she'd thought it all out: 'Champa, I want you to help me with something. I want to drive to my old middle school today to see my head teacher. It's an appointment I made ages ago, and he's leaving the country soon, so I can't put it off. The school's a long way away, somewhere near Langfang City in Hebei province. I haven't got the energy to drive myself there and back. Will you go with me and drive me back?'

'Of course I will,' I said. 'I'll drive you there and back if you like.'

Something suddenly occurred to me as we were driving along: 'Are you going to see your old head teacher to find out who your father is?'

Shell nodded. She didn't ask how I'd guessed.

I said earnestly: 'Shell, I don't think you were adopted.'

She nodded again.

I really wanted to carry on talking with Shell: 'I know you don't look much like her, but I can see a lot of similarities in your body language.' As soon as the words were out of my mouth, I felt I'd gone too far in mentioning her and her mum's bodies in the same breath.

There was a pause, then Shell said: 'Champa, please, please, when I've seen the head teacher, don't ask me what we talked about, OK? I'll tell you as soon as I feel up to it.'

I waited outside the school. It was over an hour before Shell came out. Her face was expressionless, except that she looked tired. She got into the back seat and lay down with her knees pulled up and her hands clasping her stomach. 'Champa, I need to lie down for a bit,' she said.

She stayed like that all the way back to Tongzhou and our dog kennel.

She lay down all evening, wearing the same skirt as she'd worn all day. She didn't want anything to eat but drank the glass of water I gave her and said, 'Thank you.' Then she went to the bathroom, changed into some jogging pants and lay down to sleep.

20

It was the day she said we should split up that Shell really sat down and had a proper conversation with me.

She took me to a trendy Hunan restaurant, also in Tongzhou, run by an artist. We ate lunch in an open-air courtyard. The day was bright and clear and it was pleasantly cool. There were no other customers and the waiters didn't bother us. The one waitress who hung around must have been love-struck because all afternoon she kept playing and replaying schmaltzy songs. There was Fay Wong singing 'Date' in Cantonese, and Nicholas Tse singing 'I love because I love' in Mandarin.

'This is the best time in Beijing, too early for the summer mosquitoes,' said Shell. 'It'll soon be over though.'

Shell talked. The business of the school-leaving certificate, which came up during their argument in Lhasa, had reminded her that her mum had all the right connections, and one of them was Shell's old head teacher. It occurred to Shell that her old head was also from Nanjing so must have had a special kind of relationship with Plum. That was why Shell had been able to graduate from middle school without actually getting the grades. So the head must know what Plum did back in her Nanjing days, and probably also who Shell's father was. On that basis, Shell played her hand.

After she got back to Beijing from Lhasa, she made an appointment with the school head. The man was back at the school after a long spell in Nanjing, and was due to leave for the States to see his daughter almost immediately.

When Shell got to the head's office yesterday, the man's wife was there. The head was wary: Shell had been a school dropout, a real rebel, and the head had no idea why she was here to see him, so he had his wife sit in with them. However, he relaxed a little when he saw how respectable she looked now.

Shell told the head that after leaving school she'd gone to an art and design college, and had been working as a designer ever since. She succeeded in winning his confidence, and his wife went off saying she had work to do, though she deliberately left the door open.

As soon as the woman had gone, Shell broached the subject of her father. Who was he? she asked.

The head was emphatic that he didn't know.

'If you don't tell me who my father was,' said Shell, 'I'll tell everyone that when I was a student here, you sexually molested me and that was why I never got my grades and dropped out.'

'Don't you even think of saying anything like that!' exclaimed the man, horrified.

Shell pulled at her top: 'And I'll undo my clothes and say you tried to rape me again today!'

At that, the head gave in. 'OK, OK! I'll tell you whatever you want to know, just so long as you behave yourself.'

She had obviously reverted, in his eyes, to being the problem student of old, all ready to make merry hell.

He told her then that he had been at teacher-training college with her father, and that after qualifying, they taught at the same middle school. Plum was in the first year of teacher training when the two young men were about to graduate. She had been a star student. She was bright and she was beautiful, and all the men were after her, but out of all of them, it was the head's friend that she went for. In fact, Plum had pursued him, and the courtship had happened under the head's very nose.

'I'll show you a picture of Lin,' said the head. He got out their graduation photograph and pointed to a handsome young man with a long, thin face, who looked exactly like Shell. Then the head got out the school magazine and some holiday photos of the two friends.

Shell looked at them. 'Was my father gay?' she asked.

The head frowned. 'You young people nowadays, you can see it just from looking at a few pictures. But back then, we studied and worked and lived together and I had absolutely no idea. Not for years. We just didn't know about things like that.

'Your mother didn't know either, when she was chasing him,' he went on. 'Lin was really handsome and all the girls were after him. None of them had any success, until your mum came along and got him. It was rumoured that she made him drunk, slept with him and got pregnant. Well, that's just rumour, I don't know if there's any truth in it. Soon after they were married, Lin went off to Shanghai to a teachers' conference. That was in the early '90s. Apparently, he was seduced by a foreign man and realized that he was gay. He asked Plum for a divorce so he could leave China with his lover. Your mum hoped that if he stayed around till the birth he might change his mind but Lin was adamant. As soon as you were born, he divorced Plum and was off. Back in those days, no one turned down an opportunity to go abroad.

'Your mum left Nanjing for Beijing and cut all contacts with her hometown.

'I got a job in Beijing because my wife had a Beijing resident's permit, then I transferred here. I lost contact with your mum, until years later she turned up out of the blue and asked me to take you into the upper middle school. I said yes. We'd been at the same college and were old friends. Besides I had a lot of sympathy for her. It can't have been easy for her to leave you with her parents in Nanjing and go off all on her own to Beijing. However, you were a terrible student. You dropped out and didn't even come back for your final exams. You shouldn't have got your school-leaving certificate, but your mum came and wept all over me and I gave in and fixed you up with one.'

Shell was silent for a moment. 'Now I understand,' she said. 'Thank you, sir, thank you for everything you've done for me. I can put it all behind me and live my life now.'

'But what's so shocking about being gay?' I said. 'Why didn't Plum want to talk about it?'

'Things were different back then. People were very naïve. My mum could never, in her wildest dreams, have imagined she'd end up with a homosexual. When she found out, she must have felt very foolish and then got furious. She'd been so strong, ever since she was small. It was hard to admit that, just for once, she'd made a mistake. It was totally humiliating.

'So she left too. She thought she could draw a line under the past and make a fresh start. And she nearly succeeded. She scrubbed my father right out of our lives. Only then I started to badger her about him.

'It's not important to me that my dad was gay and maybe my mum doesn't care now either. But she was adamant right from the start that she wouldn't mention his name again. That was the way she coped, or thought she had.

'When all's said and done, I haven't been completely fair to my mum,' she finished. There was that inscrutable expression on her face again; this time it looked like pain.

Suddenly, without warning, Shell changed the subject. She said very firmly: 'Champa, we've got to finish this. We're not right for each other. It's not going to work out even if we keep on trying. It's my fault, I led you on, I don't know what I was thinking of. I know now I should never have done it, and I don't want to drag it out any longer. Will you forgive me?

'We should end it now,' she went on, sounding agitated. 'That's the only way we can start over and live the kind of lives we should be living.'

Then she seemed to think of something else: 'Honestly, it really was my fault. That's what I wanted to say, Champa. I'm really sorry, honestly.'

I didn't say anything. I didn't know how to put my feelings into words. In some way, I knew this was going to happen but she'd given me so much, and I hadn't had the chance to thank her. I felt she had nothing to apologize for. She had been so open and honest. Still, I'd always done the dumping before. Those Fay Wong and Nicholas Tse tracks seemed to be on a continuous loop in my head. Weird.

We sat there until evening, both of us quite quiet. Shell had a few more things to tell me. Tying up loose ends . . . in that respect she was like her mother.

She told me she'd spoken to her 'Uncle An'. She didn't tell him we were splitting up so, as a favour to her, he'd agreed to find me some security guard work. Just so long as we didn't let Plum know. In fact, he'd already thought of a job somewhere on the outskirts of Beijing, guard duties which would suit me down to the ground, he'd said.

We spent our last night together in the dog kennel. The next day, Shell was going to move her stuff to the room in the city centre that woman was renting to her. 'Take the Tara with you,' I told her. 'I don't need it any more.' She responded with a grunt, then dropped off to sleep as if, having said all she had to say, it had given her peace of mind.

Shell, I miss you already. I miss those days in the dog kennel in this alien land.

I was in a strange, half-asleep, half-awake state, sort of day-dreaming. All this new stuff I'd picked up, the kind of stuff you didn't talk about during the daytime, was going round and round in my head.

. . . I burn with desire for you, you burned yourself for my sake, my Bodhisattva, my goddess of mercy, my healer, you're sweet dew and refreshing rain to me . . . only you can tame my demons and keep me in line, you carried me across a raging torrent, led me by that little guy of mine away from Lhasa and Plum, all the way to Beijing, driving me on in pursuit of my dream, even though this dream was so beautiful that it had to end in disappointment. You burned yourself to save me, used up all the little strength you had and asked for nothing in return, you gave me all you had. You really are the goddess of mercy incarnate. In those few days when you set yourself on fire, a small miracle occurred: the flames consumed your demons, your self-indulgence. It was as if you peeled off layers of skin, dissolving your *karma* and setting yourself free. I was at your side as you burned. If there was any way I could give something back to you, it was by staying with you while you burned. That was our destiny. But not even the Bodhisattva is omnipotent, much less you. You ferried me across the raging torrent but I'm still facing a vast ocean. I can't rely on your protection now. I have to rely on myself. But have I really got the strength to do that? I'm just a naked human life, just one of those midges, rushing to Beijing to seize my one chance to perform the mating dance.

Then I thought, there was no passion without pain, maybe I'd be lucky, maybe the Bodhisattva would protect and bless me, maybe there'd be another miracle, and maybe all living beings were just midges, and we would all create new life through the dance, providing we could avoid being annihilated. We Tibetans are dreamers.

Chapter Six

1

A JOB ON THE outskirts of Beijing, as a security guard.

I was going to work in a hotel off the southbound carriage-way of the Fourth Ring Road, south side. I suppose this was the city outskirts though it didn't look much like a city. There were a few low buildings scattered around, warehouses and clothing factories, as well as some scrap-metal dealers and car-repair work-shops. Not far off, alongside an abandoned railway line, there was a shantytown which probably housed migrant workers, 'outlanders' as the Beijingers called them, and some tower blocks. Closer to the hotel was a police station and the Reception Centre run by the National Bureau of Petitioners' Grievances, where petitioners from all over China with a complaint to present were detained before being handed to the regional authorities' Beijing staffers who, in their turn, arranged for them to be sent back home.

It was an early summer evening when I arrived, and the midges and mozzies were out in force. The cunning bastards went for my hands and face but I kept slapping at them, and I scored a hit every time.

The hotel where I reported for work was a converted ware-house. The main building was shaped like a firewood basket; it was two stories high with a smaller basement. I had a room on the ground floor, which I shared with two fellow guards.

We had no uniform, didn't shout slogans or do army drills and were not acting as security guards for the hotel. But our base was the hotel, because our security company rented its premises. We had two types of work, either off-site jobs or looking after people on-site.

Apparently we didn't work off-site every day. In fact, the first two days, we spent all our time indoors. I hoped we'd go out on a job soon; I didn't like hanging around indoors all day.

My boss was A-Li, the man with the two front teeth capped with rose-gold who'd punched me in the ribs at the dog kennels. When I first reported in, he said there were only three rules for anyone who worked with him: obey his orders, never stare at him (he hated that) and . . . he couldn't tell me what the third rule was. I thought just the second rule would be hard enough because he was always baring his teeth in a grin or a grimace and it was hard not to stare at those gold-capped gnashers.

A-Li's room faced south, and his window looked out on to the back yard. The three of us had a room opposite, facing on to the road.

'Is this part of Mr An's security business?' I asked. He didn't answer then, but later he explained that our outfit carried out ad-hoc 'Domestic Security' jobs, which Mr An passed on to A-Li. We didn't get our national insurance paid but board and lodging was included and the work wasn't hard. Every Monday, An's bookkeeper brought the cash over and paid us, and any off-site jobs earned a bonus. An easy sort of life, like oddjobbing, I thought to myself.

I was sharing with the two guys who had pinioned me when they burst into the kennels. They were brothers, big burly Chinese blokes. They were called One Circle and Two Circle, I suppose because they liked their *mahjong*. They said they were Beijingers, but their accent was so guttural I had a hard job understanding them. They told me they were here because their elder sister had slept with Mr An. That guaranteed them an 'iron rice bowl' job, so I shouldn't mess with them. They chain-smoked in the room, they stank, and they spent hours picking their noses and their toes. They had pushed their beds together and, the first evening I was there, they put a porn DVD on and lay there jerking off.

My own bed was piled high with the clothes and other oddments which had belonged to the previous occupant. It looked like he'd left in too much of a hurry to take them with him. The whole bed was in a disgusting state, covered in fag ends and ash. I asked One Circle and Two Circle who had the bed before me. They smirked, then said: 'An outlander.' They put on phoney dialect voices which they seemed to find hilariously funny.

'Is he coming back for this stuff?' I asked.

'No,' said One Circle, and Two Circle added: 'No way will that idiot be back.'

It was my job to go down to the basement and open the iron door which led to the detention room at one end so the hotel staff could deliver the food. That was the rule, said A-Li. There had to be one of us responsible for unlocking the iron door, then shutting it and locking up again after the food had been delivered. I was the rookie guard, so that person would be me.

It was dark down in the basement. To reach it, you went down a staircase with a door at the top and the bottom. The top one had a notice on: 'Staff Only'.

The first morning I went down at eleven o'clock with the hotel manager. At the bottom of the stairs, there was a corridor with the iron door at one end. I opened it to let him in with the food. Just then, the stick-like figure of a woman crawled out of the room. The manager tipped the food into a plastic bowl on the floor in front of her then deliberately kicked it over, before sauntering off down the corridor with a self-satisfied grin at me. I locked up after him as A-Li had instructed me. I was still standing there when I heard the woman say: 'Are you new here?'

I looked through a crack in the door and saw the woman sitting on the floor, looking in my direction. She was smirking as if she really could see me through the crack. Her face was all beaten up, which made her smile look very odd. She looked about forty or fifty years old, but her hair was completely white and she was missing some front teeth. 'I always know when there's a new guy on the job,' she said, still smiling, as she cleared up her dinner and put it back in the bowl, 'because he kicks the bowl over. He's just telling you to treat me as roughly as he does. But don't you go behaving like them, I can see you're a nice guy. Most people are.' I stepped back and turned to go upstairs. She had a wheedling, little-girl voice, so much at odds with her appearance that it was frightening. 'Are you off?' she said. She must have seen the light change through the door crack. 'Let's talk again this evening. Why don't you tell me your name?' I walked away without answering.

So these were the 'security duties' that Mr An thought would suit me down to the ground? Was I really going to do this work? Of course. If I didn't, what else would I do? I couldn't turn the job down on my first day. Shell hadn't been keen to approach her uncle An for me and I couldn't let her think she'd wasted her time. I would show her she hadn't put herself out for nothing and I, Champa, could stand on my own feet in Beijing. That was my second ambition. My first, as I said, was to drive all the way to Beijing from Lhasa, and I'd done that. Now I'd got this security job.

I'd never had to worry about where the next meal was coming from or about not having enough clothes. But I was in an alien land now and I knew life was going to be tough.

Still, I couldn't be too fussy. If I put my back into it and worked hard, I'd be able to stand on my own feet in Beijing and realize my dreams. I'd pull myself up by my bootstraps. If I started with this security work I'd get to know a lot of people and one day someone would recognize my worth and I'd get my chance. Someone would put me in charge of a nightclub, a bar, a disco, a karaoke bar, even a fast-food outlet. I'd put in my own money and show films, play music, sign up some live acts, and promote Tibetan arts to the whole wide world. Beijingers would lap it up. All the capital's celebs would drop in and tell me how great I was. Of course, I knew that not all my dreams would come true, but it was only human to have aspirations. And I'd fallen on my feet. Mr An must have plenty of contacts in Beijing, I'd make a good impression on him and he'd begin to value me. True, I hadn't had a chance to see him yet because he'd dumped me in this outfit of A-Li's.

At half past five, I went down to unlock the iron door again. The woman was already waiting, sitting on the floor behind it. She looked as if she'd brushed her hair and put clean clothes on. She saw me and, ignoring the manager, said: 'Let's be friends, kid!' The manager tipped her dinner – steamed bun with pickled mustard root and a small sausage – into her bowl and turned on his heel. I re-locked the door and followed him.

'Why is it always you who brings the meals?' I asked him.

'The staff refuse to do it, so I have to,' he said.

'Why don't they want to?'

'They're scared of that god-botherer.'

I didn't know what he meant by that. 'Who is she?' I asked.

The manager was suddenly wary. 'We just take care of the catering,' he said. 'We don't get involved in our clients' business.'

We ate our evening meal in the hotel staff canteen. A-Li fetched his food and took it back to eat in his own room. I'd eaten in the canteen yesterday, but I was disgusted by One Circle and Two Circle's table manners so I took my dinner back to my room too. A-Li saw me from the room opposite and waved at me to join him.

'You can't stand those dumb idiots, eh?'

I just kept quiet, not daring to look at him, let alone answer.

'I don't mind bad guys,' he said. 'Because no one's badder than me. What scares me is stupid guys trying to be bad.'

I nodded, but kept eating my dinner.

'But don't rile them,' he warned me. 'Wanna know why?'

'Because their elder sister sleeps with Mr An,' I said. I looked up to find A-Li staring at me, and quickly dropped my eyes again. I found A-Li a bit scary.

'The women in that family wash Mr An's dick every day and I'm in charge of the rota!' he said scornfully. 'The reason I told you not to mess with the brothers is because you're all my respon-sibility, get it? Idiot!'

Finally, on the third day, we had an off-site job to do. The four of us split ourselves between two Sonatas with no number plates, and set off in convoy after a police special unit Jeep Grand Cherokee, also without number plates. We got to a housing estate off the fifth ring road where we waited nearly an hour until finally a man in his fifties and a slightly younger woman came out. Two of the special unit pinioned the man by his arms, while One Circle and Two Circle got him by the legs and stuffed him into the Cherokee where two investigators were waiting to hood him.

A-Li and I took charge of the woman. We twisted her arms so far up her back, her whole body was bowed forwards. She screamed in pain, then begged us: 'I can't move, please don't be so rough, I won't resist.' A-Li glanced over at me and we relaxed our grip a little. She stayed bent over, just as she had said. The investigators' Cherokee drove off and A-Li said to the woman: 'Don't move.' We let her go and went back to our car. The woman was too terrified to straighten up.

And that was how the off-site jobs went – we were there to back up the special unit, and we got a bonus too.

The special unit men deposited the man in a cell at the other end of the basement and the brothers were put in charge of him. For the first few days, the unit staff were all in and out of the man's room. They took over a couple of other offices and store-rooms in that wing too, all windowless.

Over dinner, I asked: 'Why have the special unit brought the man here instead of the police station?'

'They've got him under what's called Residential Surveillance and it's perfectly legal in China,' said A-Li with authority. 'Originally, it meant detention in your own home but now we put them somewhere their families can't find them, usually in a hotel leased by Domestic Security, like this one. You wanna know why we don't send them direct to the police station, idiot? I'll tell you why. Once they're in the police station, formal legal proceedings have to be started which, strictly speaking, means interrogating, taping and filming the suspect. So you can't torture a confession out of them. So first they bring them to a hotel like this, and you lot give them a going-over and they confess and all the investigations are done right here. After that, the special unit go through the motions of recording the confession and send them to the police station, or they bail them, or let them go . . . it just depends.

'Have you seen anyone cuffed up?' he went on.

'What do you mean, cuffed up?'

'They're handcuffed. Then they're strung up by the handcuffs from the doorframe. Or they're made to stand bent over facing the wall with their arses stuck up in the air as a punishment. That's called being bow-strung. These are all standard methods to quench your ardour and bring you into line. Have you seen that?'

'I've never been to look. One Circle and Two Circle are in charge of that wing.'

'Them!' he said scornfully. 'They'd like nothing better than to be sent in to beat up the detainees.'

But you don't dare fire them, I thought to myself. Is that because they're under Mr An's protection?'

'Do you know why I want you to keep an eye on that woman?' And he answered himself: 'If it was One Circle and Two Circle, they'd beat her to a pulp.'

'What's wrong with her feet?' I asked.

'Broken bones!' he told me. 'But it wasn't our people who did it, it was the lot who arrested her before.'

'Why?'

'I can't tell you that. We're security,' he explained. 'We don't do interrogations. We stick to our job and don't get involved in anyone else's.'

'Why don't they let her go?'

'Idiot! Why would they let her go, now she's been so badly beaten? She's got a mouth in her head, she might talk! The people who got rough with her have been promoted several grades since then, some of them might even be senior officials, who wants to risk getting in their bad books by letting her go? Everyone's lost interest in her case by now, that's for sure. Besides, the state puts a lot of money into Domestic Security. If all the detainees were let go, they wouldn't need us, would they?'

When the manager brought the food down the next day and I had seen him out, I locked the door behind us and stood outside. She knew I was there and started going on about how I should be a good man and not follow their bad example, and so on and so forth. As I listened, it reminded me of a spoof *Journey to the West* film I'd seen, where the saintly monk keeps spouting homilies. I was beginning to find it annoying.

Before I went back up, I bumped into a waitress who was taking lunch down to the cell in the other wing. It looked a bit better than what the woman got, there was a stir-fry, and soup and a drink. I followed her down the corridor, keeping my distance, until Two Circle opened the cell door, and I saw the waitress go in and serve the food properly at the table. One of the special unit people went in too, then came out with a set of plastic cuffs. It was too dark inside to make out much and I couldn't see the man. Maybe he'd been cuffed up. Two Circle appeared in the doorway and I left, as I didn't want them to catch me watching.

I don't know what A-Li did all day. He didn't seem to have any vices – he didn't smoke or drink. On slack afternoons, he sat in the courtyard looking out towards the west, and he went to bed early at night. He seemed quite content with life.

I spent the evening playing games on my iPad, but once I shouted out: 'Yeah! Gimme five!', the brothers turned the TV volume up to maximum. I remembered A-Li telling me not to rile them and I didn't fancy hanging around in the room with them either, so I took a stroll outside the hotel. I got as far as the shantytown. There had been a thunderstorm that afternoon and, though the rain had stopped now, the shantytown roads were all muddy. It was a lively place. There were half a dozen stalls catering to the outlanders who worked in nearby factories and warehouses, and offering snacks from all over China by the smell of them. To my surprise, there were little clusters of girls standing at the roadside, some of them astonishingly young. I couldn't believe I was in Beijing. There were a couple of small supermarkets too. Too bad they shut early, otherwise I could have got some wine from them. I'd come out earlier another day, I thought. I bought a bottle of Yanjing beer from a stall and sat down at the roadside watching the hookers bargaining with the punters, then leading the way to wherever they had their rooms, somewhere nearby I suppose. I felt at peace. My life seemed to be moving along nicely, but not too fast. I drank three big bottles of beer before going back to the hotel when the stallholder packed up. By the time I got back to my room, the brothers were snoring. I groped my way to the bed and realized they'd turned it upside down.

We went out on another off-site job and A-Li told me to drive one of the Sonatas. We parked up on a slip road to the Beijing–Hong Kong Highway and waited. Then a minibus with a dozen or so passengers appeared in the distance. A-Li yelled at One Circle and Two Circle in the other car, through an old-fashioned walkie-talkie: 'Stop clowning around, you two, get ready!'

As the minibus passed us, One Circle shot out in front of it, and A-Li put on the Sonata's siren and told me to drive after it and not to lose it, whatever I did. One Circle was a nifty driver and, once he'd pulled in front of the minibus, he kept speeding up and slowing down. The passengers must have been getting car sick and the terrified minibus driver was forced to slam on the brakes. One Circle and Two Circle jumped out of their car and started to harangue the driver. A-Li and I got out too and waited for the door of the minibus to open.

'You get on first and punch anyone who makes any fuss, OK?' A-Li instructed me. I nodded and psyched myself up for the fray. When the bus door opened, I leapt on board. An old man in the front row made as if to get to his feet but I hit him and he slumped down again. In the second row, a small boy gave a yell and I leaned over and gave him a straight left. The woman beside him tried to protect him and, without thinking, I swiped her with my right fist. Then an old woman shouted from the back row: 'Don't hit us! We'll go home! Don't keep hitting us!'

After landing three blows, my fists were sore. I looked down the bus – there were about twenty passengers, all of them old folk plus some children, all cringing in fear in their seats, not daring to move. I looked at the boy. Blood was trickling from his mouth but he was too frightened to cry.

I turned round and saw A-Li and the brothers standing by the driver's seat and in the doorway, with grins on their faces. All three had coshes in their hands. 'So you still use your fists, eh?' said A-Li. The other two pointed at me and roared with laughter.

A-Li struck the metal frame of a seat with his cosh: 'Don't let me see any of you in Beijing again!'

The old woman at the back piped up at that: 'No, sir, we'll go home now, we promise!'

With a wave of the cosh, A-Li got off the bus and we followed him.

After this, A-Li was even keener for me to have dinner in his room. The brothers must have been jealous but they left me well alone. Once they were walking along with A-Li and I saw A-Li hold his nose when they weren't looking. I did a bad thing at dinner, I said they stank. A-Li said: 'They're country folk, not townies like us. Their standards of hygiene are lower than ours, right?'

I liked it when A-Li made derogatory comments about the brothers. In fact, I liked talking to him. I was learning a lot from him.

'Which are the world's three biggest capital cities, do you know?' he quizzed me one day.

I said I didn't.

'Beijing, Urumqi and Istanbul!' he said.

'Have you been to all of them?'

'I haven't been to Istanbul yet. I'm saving up until I've got enough money to move there,' he said. 'Istanbul is absolutely the world's greatest capital city!' He was suddenly fired with enthusiasm. 'Take a look at the map. It's right at the heart of Asia, Africa and Europe. That puts it at the heart of the world. Istanbul is the real Middle Kingdom!'

Well, Tibet's called the Earth's 'third pole', I thought to myself, so if Istanbul is the heart of the Middle Kingdom, then Lhasa is the heart of the Heavenly Kingdom. And I began to feel homesick.

'How much money do you need?' I asked A-Li.

He shook his head and grunted. He said there had been loads more off-site jobs a few years ago and he'd made a lot on bonuses. A-Li's outfit provided back-up when the provincial authorities' staffers in Beijing moved to intercept local petitioners. And they were also needed when there were too many Domestic Security operations for the central government to cope with. At one time, they'd had several off-site jobs in one day. The security company, which belonged to the Boss (that is, Shell's 'Uncle An'), had leased several hotels to detain the petitioners in. But then a weekly magazine in Guangzhou did an exposé on what they called 'Beijing's black jails' and there was a change in policy. The government was hiring people direct now and there were too many security companies all fighting over the same small piece of Domestic Security cake. He couldn't make as much money as he used to. He licked his gold teeth. Maybe he'd just go straight to Istanbul, he said, if he couldn't make enough in Beijing.

He'd been fifteen years in Urumqi, and another fifteen years in prison in China, and the plan was to work and save for fifteen years in Beijing, then go to Istanbul. He'd arrived here at fifteen years old, and worked as a young hitman for a crime syndicate, until the Boss caught him. Now he was the Boss's partner, responsible for the team that carried out ad-hoc Domestic Security jobs.

I probed a bit: 'Have you really killed people?'

'Maybe I have, maybe I haven't,' he said craftily.

'Well, have you?' I persisted.

He curled up his upper lip, showing his gold teeth, then started on another lecture. 'Think about it this way: you're walking around outside at night, and I come up behind you with a knife and kill you and take your ID card, what do you think's going to happen? I'm telling you, nothing. Nothing's going to happen to me. If someone like you, an outlander, a nobody with no family in Beijing and no job here, dies, do you think it's ever going to come to court? Not a chance. Ten-to-one, it'll be put down as an accident or a suicide, and no one will bother to investigate. That's why there are so many cases of "suicides" and "accidents", and hardly any murders. Even if it is a suspected murder, there'll be no media coverage or investigation by the special units. They only deal with cases they can solve. If they can't solve it, they don't bother asking any questions. After a while, they pick some poor sod they can pin a whole bunch of cases on, whether he did it or not, and – bingo – all the cases are solved in one fell swoop, and the investigator gets a bonus. That's why the clear-up rate is so high. Almost all these cases end in a conviction. So when the police say they've cracked a case, the accused is almost bound to get banged up. Do you understand?'

I nodded.

'What I'm getting at,' he went on complacently, 'is that anyone can kill someone like you and get away with it. The killer won't be held criminally responsible. Your life is worth tuppence. If you die, it's just an accidental death, or a suicide. If they fit you up, then you did it; if they say you've committed so many crimes, then that's the number you've committed. And you'll get the death penalty!' And he roared with laughter.

He glanced at me: 'In fact, you're the ideal person to fit up!' Another jovial burst of laughter.

Then he looked sombre. 'That's how it is . . . no different for me either. If I died in a ditch, no one would look into my death. But if anyone comes to get me, I'm gonna hammer them first. They squeeze my balls, I'm gonna mash theirs first. Several lives for the price of one. Mine's worth it. As for yours, you better go and beg your Buddha for eyes in the back of your head.' He guffawed again.

For the whole evening after our talk, I was too depressed to go to the shantytown. But by the second day, I'd put it all out of my mind.

The last couple of days, whenever I opened up the iron door, the god-botherer started shouting: 'I want greens, give me some greens with my dinner, I'm bunged up, I need greens!' The manager ignored her, turned on his heel and left. She stopped shouting then and began to wheedle. 'Do you have a faith?' she asked me. 'Are you married? Got a sweetheart?' I didn't answer, just went out and locked the door behind me.

That evening at dinner, I asked A-Li: 'That woman in the basement, how much do we pay for her dinner?'

A-Li shrugged. 'Ask the Boss's bookkeeper.'

'She keeps shouting she wants greens. All she gets every day is sausage and pickled mustard root with rice or a steamed bun.'

'I don't know what the state meal allowance is, but however measly it is, someone's going to want to take a cut of it. Understand me, idiot?' Then he pointed his finger in my face. 'You should just mind your own business!'

The next evening, when I went down the steps with the manager, he had a face like thunder and ignored my greeting. I noticed he was carrying an extra dish, a saucer full of stir-fried oilseed rape. So A-Li had had a word with him.

The god-botherer started shouting that she wanted greens as soon as she heard us coming. Then she saw the saucer and gave a cry of delight.

The manager tipped the food into her plastic bowl on the floor as usual and kicked it over. Suddenly I lost it. I grabbed his shirt-front, and he squealed: 'What are you doing?' Then I saw the god-botherer watching us so I let him go. I re-locked the door and the manager walked away giving me a black look. I heard the god-botherer from inside: 'I know you spoke up for me so I got the greens today. Thank you, young man. You're my knight in shining armour. It is more blessed to give than to receive! All thanks to you, I'm looking at something green for the first time in ages.' It was on the tip of my tongue to say that A-Li had put in a word for her, but something told me I should leave it at that. I went back upstairs again.

On the Monday morning, the bookkeeper turned up and I got my pay – a wad of hundred-*yuan* notes. After lunch, A-Li and the brothers were going out. He beckoned to me, and I went along too.

One Circle drove for an hour or so. As we crossed into Hebei province, I asked: 'Where are we going?'

The brothers chorused: 'The ten-*yuan* place.'

'For a fuck!' added Two Circle.

'But there are places like that in the shantytown.'

'It's ten *yuan* a fuck and no need for a condom,' said Two Circle.

We got to a small town and stopped at a hotel. Upstairs, the first and second floors were all divided into cubicles. Most had their doors open. The windows were blacked out and the only light came from a bedside light bulb wrapped in a red plastic bag. Most of the space was taken up with a single bed, each with a girl sitting on it. It was too dark to see what they looked like, but A-Li, One Circle and Two Circle quickly made their choice and went inside. I wandered up to the second floor. A woman came out into the corridor and said: 'I haven't been with anyone today, I'm clean, no need for a condom.' I let myself be led into her room. She was rough-looking and in her forties, and in the past I would have said she looked too rough, but at least it was the sort of rough look I was used to – in fact she reminded me of my two elder sisters and my mum. Fuck it! What on earth am I doing here? I thought.

'Give me fifty,' she said. I counted the fifty out and gave it to her.

I waited for A-Li and the brothers at the entrance to the hotel. The punters going in and out all seemed to be older men. I was worried I might not be back in time to take the food downstairs at 5.30. Finally, after more than an hour, the three of them came out.

'Been out long, have you?' asked One Circle.

I knew if I told them the truth they'd take the piss out of me, so I said I'd just come out.

'How much did you spend?' asked Two Circle.

'Fifty.'

They sneered. 'We only paid ten.'

'The stupid bitch enjoyed it so much she didn't want paying, I had to force it on her,' added Two Circle.

As the brothers carried on their bragging, A-Li said to me behind their backs: 'Those idiots.' He must have seen me looking at my watch because he added: 'She won't starve to death.'

The traffic was snarled up on the way back and it was past seven by the time we got to the hotel. I hurried down to the basement. The food was sitting outside the iron door, covered in flies. I heard the god-botherer from behind the door: 'I knew you wouldn't forget me. Is anything up, lad?'

I found myself saying: 'Hang on a moment.'

I ran up the stairs and got a steamed bun, some pickled mustard and sausage, and a saucer of stir-fried vegetables from the staff canteen. A-Li and the brothers were standing at the food counter. Back down the steps, I opened up and was just about to take the dishes in when they were snatched out of my hand. I turned round. It was A-Li, looking as ferocious as I'd ever seen him. He ordered me to tip the fly-blown food into the god-botherer's bowl.

She smiled at me: 'Thank you, lad, I appreciate your kindness.' A-Li glared pointedly at the door and I locked up behind us. Still glowering, he dumped the bowl of fresh food on the floor and stalked off without a word.

The god-botherer was rabbiting on, begging me to give her the food A-Li had thrown to the ground outside, but I ignored her. I scraped it up, wiped the ground with an old cleaning rag and went back upstairs.

2

That was the low point of the day. Just then, I received a couple of texts.

The first – I had no idea who it was from – went:

So long as the universe endures and life persists, the youth of the waterfall will never wane and the waterfall of youth will never fade. A torch flares like the full moon, we will have failed but we will not weep.

I puzzled over it until it made me dizzy. Half an hour later, I got another text from the same number. 'I've finally got the hang of this mobile, and I'm learning how to text.' It was Nyima, the hitch-hiker I'd given a ride to on my way to Beijing.

He was just the sort of person to send nonsense texts. I ignored them.

I must have been mad, fetching food for the god-botherer from the staff canteen. That was a step too far. It had made A-Li angry. He'd think I was on her side and was unreliable. I wanted to keep in A-Li's good books but now I'd messed up. He'd think I was stupid, and he didn't like stupid people, especially not stupid and unreliable people.

I got a text from Shell in the afternoon: 'I went to see my mum. She was in Beijing for a minor op. We had a good chat, about my dad too. I feel quite emotional, and happy. Hope all is well with you! Shell.'

Ah, so Shell's made it up with her mum, I thought. Then another text came: 'Forgot to say I told Mum we'd split up, but I told her it was me who came on to you.'

I felt upset. Why was Shell trying to protect me and take the blame? Was she deliberately acting the goddess of mercy? Then I calmed down a bit. When it came down to it, Shell was just being kind and shielding me from her mum's anger.

I was a bit up and down that day.

At dinnertime, when I took my food back to my room, A-Li's door was shut and he didn't invite me in. The brothers knew I was out of favour and smirked.

I found myself calling Nyima's number. Maybe I just wanted someone to talk to in Tibetan.

He said he was in Beijing and we should meet up. I said it was gone eight o'clock.

'That's not late,' he said.

I thought it was. In any case, I told him, I had no car.

'Where are you?'

'Right on the edge of town, further south from Red Gate Bridge on the fourth ring road south.' He said he was looking up the buses on the web. Since when had he known how to check Beijing bus timetables on the web? 'Got it,' he said. 'You can pick up a 729 from Red Gate Bridge north, and it'll drop you at Beijing train station. I'm just checking the map – get off right in front of the train station and walk south to the south-west exit of the number 2 metro. I'll be in the McDonald's on the first floor of the shopping mall opposite.'

There was a covered passageway at the end of the main building, which took you down the side of the compound to the south building, from where I could leave by the back gate.

The south building was leased by another security company, and held a particular category of petitioners waiting to be sent home. I never found out why those petitioners weren't taken to the Reception Centre run by the National Bureau of Petitioners' Grievances, which was nearby, or maybe they'd been decanted from there and the local government Beijing staffers hadn't taken charge of them yet. These security guards only used the back entrance and didn't go near the main hotel building. I knew the south building was nearer to the shantytown, so it was a good shortcut. As I walked past the petitioners' cells, a woman called through the window bars: 'Please, sir, could I borrow your phone to make a call?' She was a good-looking woman, just my type, but I ignored her and walked on.

I took the 729 bus from outside the scrap dealers on the other side of the shantytown, and got off at Beijing train station. The main road cut through a crowded square, with branches of McDonald's on all four sides. I followed Nyima's instructions and crossed over the footbridge. There were Tibetans selling things on top and on the pavement underneath. I had no trouble finding the McDonald's on the first floor of the shopping mall in the south-west corner of the square.

Nyima was sitting by the window with a good view of Station Square. He was wearing dark glasses and occupying a table for four which was littered with half-eaten hamburgers, some chips, half-finished bottles of pop and a jumble of napkins and wrapping paper, and a touch-screen phone.

We did a knuckle-bump, like black Americans do. Nyima greeted me with a 'Yo!' and we did a high-five.

'Dark glasses at night?' I exclaimed. 'You look like a film director!'

He pushed the glasses up with his index finger. 'Didn't you know being blind is cool nowadays?'

'Rubbish!' I said.

'You must have heard of that lawyer, Chen Guangchen!' he said. 'All over the world people are talking about blind people, it's not just China!'

'Is that true?' I said. 'But can you see anything with dark glasses on at night?'

'Ah,' he said mysteriously. 'That depends on what you want to see. Like, sometimes you can get spaced out with them on, like in the film *Inner Senses*.' He fumbled for a half-eaten hamburger as if he really was blind and pushed it into his mouth. As he chewed, he said: 'Even with eyes, you can't always see much, it's no different from being half blind.'

'How much have you eaten?' I asked.

'There were four of us till just now, the other three have gone. I asked them to leave some for me. Want some?'

'I've eaten,' I said. He drank up the Coke and orange pop.

'Doesn't the train to Lhasa leave from Beijing West station?' I asked.

'This is nothing to do with getting the train. This is where we talk.'

'What are you doing in Beijing?'

'I was on my way here when you gave me a lift. I just thought you wouldn't want to take me this far, so I got out at Xining.'

'Why didn't you tell me before? And what are you doing here anyway?'

'Nothing, really. And I advise other people to do nothing too. I just meet my friends for a chat. Look, one of them gave me this.' He pointed to the mobile. 'I have to use it now I've got it.'

'Yes, you do,' I said. I couldn't figure out how Nyima was doing so well in Beijing.

'How are you getting on?' he suddenly asked.

I didn't know what to say for a moment, then I blurted out: 'Not too well.'

'A bit of a struggle, eh?'

'You can say that again. It's crap.'

I told him about Plum, and Shell, and me, and the time we spent in our dog kennel. (Of course, I didn't tell him I was Plum's Tibetan mastiff pup, or about not being able to get it up.) It all came tumbling out. It was as if I was rehearsing the story I'd tell other people afterwards. Nyima, still with his dark glasses on, listened impassively. I had no idea if he was taking it in, or if his thoughts were wandering off somewhere completely different.

I'd never talked so much in my life. I went on and on, it was like talking into a black hole. A couple of times I saw Nyima's lips tremble slightly as if he was reciting the sutras.

'I'm not keeping you from your work, am I?' I said.

'I don't have any work. I never have any proper work. I already checked online, the first 729 leaves at six in the morning. This is a 24-hour McDonald's, so you can carry on talking.'

I looked at my watch. It was nearly midnight and the last 729 back to the shantytown had gone. I was worried, then I thought, what am I worried about? I had no desire to go back to that three-man dog kennel. I might as well hang out in this 24-hour McDonald's. When it got light, I'd see.

'Let me get spaced out!' I said. 'Lend me your dark glasses.'

Nyima took another pair from his backpack. I put them on, but didn't feel anything particular.

I went to buy two Big Macs, and ordered a Coke and a coffee, and got chicken wings and a vanilla shake for Nyima. Something to eat and drink to see us through the night. It hadn't been easy to get away from the hotel. Why not enjoy it?

Nyima pointed mysteriously at another table, at some weird-looking youths. 'A gang of pickpockets,' he said.

'How do you know?'

'When the evening rush-hour's over, they knock off work and come here for a snack, and count their takings,' he said. 'I spent yesterday evening watching them with my dark glasses on.'

I took a bite of the Big Mac. It tasted reassuringly familiar. I remembered the first time I'd had one: on New Year's Eve, 1999, at the Millennium Hotel in Chengdu. The whole family were there, my dad, my mum, my two elder sisters, my aunt, and me. I was just starting middle school then and one small bite was a big step in my life. The pleasure was comparable to kissing a girl on the mouth for the first time. What had happened to the good times? Why were there some feelings that vanished for ever? I kept my head down, eating my Big Mac, feeling close to tears.

It was an evening in early summer, and I was in a nice air-conditioned place, with no mosquitoes or bites. I'd been here in Beijing for a long time, but this was the first time I could really chill out. I'd been tense with Shell and the same with A-Li. But chatting nonsense with the enigmatic Nyima was different. There was no pressure. I felt as if, ever since I arrived in Beijing, I'd been cuffed up or bow-strung, and now, for the first time, the cuffs were off. I could slob around just as I liked here. Chilling out, that was what I liked.

I explained to Nyima what handcuffing and stringing up and being bent over like a bow meant. I told him about the Domestic Security hotel, about A-Li with the rose-gold teeth, and the woman in the basement cell. I asked him why they called her a god-botherer. Turned out I'd misheard and the word wasn't 'botherer' at all. Nyima wrote the proper character for me on a paper napkin and explained it meant she was a devout believer.

I told him the security work gave me board and lodging, the duties were light, the pay wasn't bad and I can't say I was treated badly. But the weird thing was, there was something that felt worse than bad treatment, and it was falling into a gutter. I didn't want to say that the hotel was worse than a kennels, I didn't want to give dogs a bad name, but this job was making me feel really stressed. I had to keep other people banged up but I felt as if the one who was banged up was me.

'Isn't that the way we all live now?' said Nyima. 'We've all got plenty to eat and drink, a place to live, and things to keep us happy, but really we're all cuffed up. And bow-strung. Within our own small domain, we can walk back and forth and look out, but if we try to go further, we can't. The only difference is that sometimes the rope that ties us up is a bit longer or a bit shorter. Anyone who's more or less human knows quite well that the only way they can live is bow-strung.'

Nyima was a clever man. He'd put into words exactly what I was feeling.

My thoughts wandered for a moment, and then I heard Nyima say: '. . . there's another trick too, it's called "support". We're all being supported, one way or another. Some people, like petty officials, local government employees and Domestic Security staff, are hand-reared. We Tibetans, we're herded. We've all become well behaved, really well behaved. If I support you, you won't dare behave badly towards me, because I'll punish you till you behave, and if you behave badly again, then I'll punish you with death.'

'Can't we decide not to play the game?' I chipped in.

'Of course we can't. If you try not to play the game, they'll play with you because you're in their way.'

I could feel myself suddenly getting very angry: 'Anyone dares play with me, I'll beat them up, I'll mash their balls!'

'It's no use beating them up,' Nyima said. 'Don't you remember the car crash we came across? The little old banger hit the big 4x4, and it had no chance, no chance at all.'

I remembered Nyima leaning over the decapitated head and whispering in its ear. I remembered the driver of the 4x4, his face spattered with the victim's blood and brains. I remembered how the little old banger had been flattened to a pancake and turned into a bloody piece of scrap iron.

I was still angry: 'I don't like being cuffed up and bow-strung, I don't want to be supported, however comfortably, I just don't like it, and that's that!'

Nyima pushed up his glasses with his index finger and said

soothingly: 'No one can be free just now, what counts is how much give there is in your rope. Hey, just hang in there, Champa. Remember, life's a bitch, but nothing lasts for ever. Good times will pass, and so will bad times.'

A bit after six in the morning, wearing the dark glasses Nyima had given me, I went off to the bus station to get the 729 back to the shantytown.

3

I got back in by the hotel's south gate, the same way I'd come out. I half hoped I'd see the good-looking woman petitioner who'd asked to borrow my phone, but she must have been transferred away during the night, I don't know where to.

I looked at the petitioners who were still there. There were men and women, old and young. Some of them had been here since before I arrived and still hadn't been sent home. Every day more petitioners were bussed in and some were bussed out. In other words, waves of petitioners arrived in Beijing every day. Where had they popped up from? Why were they so determined to leave their homes and families for Beijing? Surely they didn't really believe Beijing would welcome them with open arms? Maybe, I thought, they really had nothing to lose except their lives.

When I got back to my room, the bed had been turned upside down again. No doubt I'd annoyed One Circle and Two Circle by staying out all night.

I was not in a good place. Without the protection of A-Li, the brothers would really take it out on me. I had offended the manager too and the hotel staff would certainly listen to his side of things, not to mine, and I could expect distinctly unfriendly treatment from them.

We delivered the food at half past five, the manager left and I was just locking up when it occurred to me that it was the god-botherer who had got me into all this trouble. The woman not only had no idea I was angry with her, she was convinced I was gunning for her. Now she was holding up a roll of toilet paper, scrawled all over with characters: 'Do something for me, will you, lad? Give this to a friend of mine? I've put his name and address at the top.'

I pushed the door shut with both hands, not knowing whether to laugh or cry. In Lhasa, I behaved myself and did what the government said, I thought to myself, and in Beijing, it's my job to keep the god-botherer banged up. And still she's got the idea I'm on her side? I have to give it to her, she's persistent . . . She'd stopped speaking and something made me turn round. One Circle was standing behind me. When he saw me looking, he walked away. I picked up my dinner in the staff canteen and took it to my room. As I walked slowly past A-Li's door, I heard him say: 'I can't work magic, Boss. How do you want me to find someone and fit him up, just like that?'

Our eyes met and he hurriedly looked away. He still had the phone in one hand, and with the other he pushed the door shut. I carried on to my room to eat my dinner.

When I got there, I couldn't find my iPad. One Circle and Two Circle turned up and I said sternly: 'Where's my stuff?'

'We haven't stolen your iPad,' they said in unison. 'You can't go saying things like that without proof.'

I wanted to punch them, but this clearly wasn't the right moment. 'I'm going to talk to A-Li,' I said. I knocked lightly on his door. Behind me the brothers were yelling: 'A-Li! A-Li!'

A-Li came out without speaking. We stood in the corridor, all shouting at once.

'They've stolen my iPad!'

'He's been taking out letters for the god-botherer!'

'I have not!' I protested, frantic.

'I saw it with my own eyes!' (That was One Circle.)

'That's rubbish! I did not—!'

Suddenly A-Li's fists shot out and, in a flash, he had landed punches on all three of us. We each fell to the ground, clutching our ribs in pain. 'You've all broken the third rule!' he barked. Then he went back into his room and shut the door.

When A-Li punched me in the ribs at the kennels, it had been painful for days. Now he'd landed a second punch in the same spot. One Circle and Two Circle were glowering at me but at least their faces were screwed up in pain too.

I had a lie-in the next morning and skipped breakfast. The odd thing was that after the brothers got back, they were in high good humour, pulling idiotic faces at me. They must have been talking to A-Li about me. It seemed like they knew something that I didn't. That could only be bad news for me.

A-Li must have sent One Circle and Two Circle to search the god-botherer's cell because her face was red and swollen. I got a mouthful of abuse when I delivered her lunch: 'Some people are worse than animals. Animals behave better than humans.' She probably thought I'd shopped her, just like before she thought I'd been the one to get her greens with her meals. I was sick of the sound of her voice by then. I slammed the iron door shut and followed on the manager's heels up the stairs.

Back in the staff canteen, I realized One Circle and Two Circle weren't there having lunch. I took my food back to the room, passing A-Li's open door. There was no one inside.

I saw at once that my clothes and other belongings were all heaped on the bed, and there were fag ends and ash scattered all over them, just like the first day I arrived. This was too much. If I didn't punch those two, my name wasn't Champa.

I sat down in a rage, put on my dark glasses and looked at Nyima's last text: *So long as the universe endures and life persists, the youth of the waterfall will never wane and the waterfall of youth will never fade. A torch flares like the full moon, we will have failed but we will not weep.*

The phone rang. It was Shell. I took a deep breath and answered. 'Champa? This is Shell.'

'Hey, Shell!'

'Everything OK?'

'Fine.'

'Have you had lunch?'

'I'm just about to have it. What about you?'

'Just about to. I wanted to ask, how's the work going?'

'Fine!'

'Good.'

'Is something up?'

'No, nothing. Just that I got a call from Uncle An this morning, and he said he'd bumped into Mum and she told him we'd split. He wanted to check that was right and I said yes. He asked if I was still involved with you at all, I said no, and he said that's OK then. That reminded me I hadn't called you in ages. I just wondered how you're getting on.'

'It's nice of you to think of me,' I said.

'And I'm wondering what Uncle An's phone call was all about,' she went on. 'It was pretty odd, and I wondered if there'd been some problem at your work, that's why I'm asking. Is anything up?'

'Nothing.'

'That's good, that's all OK then.'

'Hey, Shell, thank you. Thank you very much.'

'You're welcome. Bye,' and she hung up.

I sat there puzzled for a long time. Why was the Boss asking if Shell and I were still together? Did A-Li want to sack me?

I must really have grown eyes in the back of my head, because something made me look out of the window. A police car had pulled up at the hotel entrance and three uniformed officers got out and strode inside.

I stood rooted to the spot, suddenly feeling panicky. Had they come for me? I scuttled quickly to the far end of the corridor and, keeping well hidden, peered round the corner. The police came into view. They were pausing to check the room numbers, then they charged into our room.

I went along the covered walkway to the south building, thinking I'd make my getaway by the south gate. As I passed the petitioners' cells, an old boy asked if he could borrow my phone. Without thinking, I pushed my iPhone through the bars. I regretted it straightaway. There was no need to be so generous. But I couldn't get it back now.

I left by the south gate and ran through the shantytown to the bus station by the scrap dealers. I could see a bus coming and jumped on. I got off at the next stop and changed to the number 729 at Red Gate Bridge north.

I stayed on till I got to Beijing train station, regretting being so rash. I'd lost my iPhone . . . and not just the phone but the SIM card too. I went into a shopping centre, bought a cheap mobile and a SIM, and called the only number I remembered: 'Shell, it's me, Champa. Something's up!'

It began to tip down with rain, and I stood at the side door of the shopping centre by the rubbish bins, sheltering from the rain along with the stray cats and dogs, while I waited for Shell to come and pick me up.

4

Shell collected me and we drove west, on to the motorway and southwards towards Hebei province. The rain stopped.

As soon as I was in the car, I blurted out everything that had happened, stuttering in my haste, my words tumbling over one another. I told her about the security guard work, about A-Li with the rose-gold teeth, the woman with the broken feet in the basement west wing cell, the man detained in the east wing and about the petitioners in the hotel south block. I even told her about the off-site jobs, how I got on the bus we'd stopped and punched a child, a woman and an old man. Shell was the person who understood me best in the whole wide world, and I told her everything. She began to cry as she listened, most of all, it seemed, for the god-botherer woman and those petitioners.

'What a dark place this world is!' she exclaimed. 'That things like this go on, and we don't even know!'

'I reckon I've been fitted up,' I said, 'just like the guy who did the job before me. We're all nameless and jobless, waifs and strays, with nothing to lose but our lives. Anyone can do us in, we're the ideal people to pin cases on. I need to get away, and I need your help.'

'Whatever,' said Shell, 'you're not going back there.' She sounded like she was really on my side.

When we got to the border with Hebei province, I said: 'We're here now. The Beijing police won't bother from here on, right?'

'Probably not,' said Shell, 'but you can't be sure.'

We stopped to fill up with petrol and buy some drinks. I went to have the crap I'd been holding in all afternoon. I thought of Nyima's words. They finally made sense. I've stopped dreaming, Nyima.

Now I'd lost the phone, I'd lost Nyima too. I tried to remember the lines in his text but I'd forgotten bits. I wanted to know who'd written the lines but no one could tell me that now.

Gloomily, I went back to the car. Shell was worried. 'I've just seen a tweet that a Tibetan self-immolated in front of a Beijing train station at five o'clock today.'

'Which station?' I asked anxiously.

'The one where I picked you up just past four o'clock!' said Shell.

'Let me see,' I said.

'I'm just looking,' Shell said. 'The first tweet I saw's been deleted.' But none of the search words she used turned up the post she'd first seen.

Shell made a gesture of defeat. 'I can't find it. They must be blocking it.'

It was true what Nyima said: even with eyes you can't always see much, it's no different from being half blind.

I told Shell about my trip to Beijing train station a couple of days back, and meeting Nyima in the McDonald's. He'd given me the dark glasses I had on, I said. Shell asked if the man who burnt himself to death could have been Nyima.

It suddenly flashed into my mind that Nyima said he had a death impulse. Then I burst out: 'No, it couldn't be him! He's always said that people shouldn't do anything, and he's always telling people not to pursue their dreams. How could it be him? No, no, absolutely not!' I wanted to tell Shell exactly what Nyima was like, but I couldn't get the words out.

'You went to Beijing train station the evening before last,' Shell said thoughtfully, 'and you went again today. If they check the CCTV footage, they might suspect you were involved.'

As soon as she said the words, my heart gave a lurch. It was scary that even a girl like Shell could make that connection. I knew I hadn't done anything, but if the police checked up, there'd be hell to pay!

'A good thing we left Beijing just after four o'clock. If we'd left it any later, any nearer the time of the self-immolation, they'd have put road blocks in place and we might not have got away.'

I was getting a headache. If they really wanted to interrogate me, leaving Beijing wouldn't have done me any good at all.

I was about to tell Shell to let me out at Zhuozhou City, the next one we were coming to.

But suddenly she said: 'How about you take my car and get home as fast as you can.

'Leave me at Zhuozhou train station,' she went on, 'and I'll get a train or a bus back to Beijing. Drive yourself home and we'll see about the car after that. There are two metros near where I'm living at the moment, I don't need the car. In fact, it's hard to find a parking space.'

All I could do was nod my head.

The more we drove on south, the more agitated I felt. Who had self-immolated? Why? Nyima would have known why, he understood everything. Why on earth hadn't I asked him this before? For the last few months, there had been a certain amount of gossip going around Lhasa about self-immolations but it had never occurred to me to find out more. If only Nyima was with me now, I could have asked him anything I didn't understand and he would have explained. There were so many things I wanted to ask him about, but he'd gone. Please tell me, Buddha, why do people set fire to themselves? It must be so painful! Why's the world got like this? Nyima, where are you? You always told people not to do anything, but sometimes people have nothing left to lose but their lives. What are they supposed to do? What other way is there? Someone, tell me! Oh, Nyima, I hope you got away from Beijing safely. I hope you're on the road getting lifts.

When we got to Zhuozhou train station, Shell told me to pull into the short-stay parking. We sat there gloomily, knowing we had to say goodbye.

Shell turned and smiled at me.

I tried to lighten up but found myself saying stupidly: 'Hey, Shell, why don't we drive off into the sunset. We could go anywhere we want, how about it?' As soon as I'd finished speaking I knew I sounded daft.

Shell wasn't angry with me. Instead, she said: 'Champa, I'm sorry I never really loved you and I don't think you ever really loved me either. But I want to say thank you, you made me think hard about a lot of things!'

I thought she was referring to her lesbian lover in Beijing. 'I guess you know now that you can love men,' I said. But she shook her head. 'You still love women?' I asked.

She said: 'Right now, I don't know anything any more.' She gave a puzzled laugh. 'That's what I'm thanking you for.'

I knew she still had something to say.

'All I know is I love my dogs,' she went on. 'I'll never leave them, and that's why I'm going back. We'd better say goodbye.'

I nodded.

She opened the car door and got out. I got out too.

'You go straight home. No messing around.'

I nodded again.

Then she said hesitantly: 'I told my mum that it was me who came on to you but I'm not sure she believed me. She's not a bad woman but she's dead jealous. I can't help you there. Just be careful when you get back to Lhasa.'

I felt terribly sad. I hugged her very tight.

Before she left, she said: 'The Tara statuette is in the suitcase. Take it with you.' She gave me a mischievous wink, just like her mum, just like the Tara. I felt a jolt of lightning and suddenly I was on fire.

Then, as I watched Shell go into the station, a wave of sadness hit me. I was alone now, and in a panic. I was actually beginning to shake with fear. I was afraid of staying here, I was afraid of going back to Lhasa. As tears brimmed in my eyes, I held them back, telling myself fiercely: 'Don't you dare cry, Champa, you've failed but you're not going to cry, whatever happens you're not going to cry.'

Still shaking, I got the bag out of the suitcase and unwrapped Shell's Tara statuette. I stared hard at it and the shaking gradually stopped. I focused my breathing. With every breath I was alive. I breathed, I lived, I breathed, I lived. I began to calm down. The Tara was serene, so serene.

I took a deep breath. I looked at the Tara again. I pulled myself together.

I realized how good the air felt after the rainstorm.

I had to admit the world really hadn't treated me badly.

Like, I'd got to know Shell, hadn't I?

Like, I'd met Nyima, that was something else good, I'd got to know Nyima.

And A-Li. I'd learnt a lot from him.

And then there were the animal protection volunteers. Yep, they loved dogs because they understood them. They were wrong about me because they didn't understand me. If they'd only understood me, they would have come to love me. Absolutely no doubt.

I screwed up my eyes, lifted the little bag up and reverentially pressed the Tara statuette on to the crown of my head.

I had a new dream now. I was fed up with having dreams but this one came into my head anyway.

One day, at some point far in the future, I might go on the road again. All over the land, I'd explore every corner . . . I'd meet Han Chinese, Tibetans, Uyghurs, all the peoples of China, and I'd really have a good time. I'd chill out, I'd get to make friends with all of them, and I'd keep learning. That was the life I liked. And maybe one day I'd even get my own passport and I'd travel the world, chilling out, learning new things and making new friends. That's right, just so long as the universe endured and life persisted, that would be my dream.

But the first thing to do was to carry the Tara back home and give it to my gran. She'd like it.

Chan Koonchung was born in Shanghai and raised in Hong Kong. He was a reporter at an English newspaper in Hong Kong before he founded the influential *City Magazine* in 1976, where he was publisher for twenty-three years. He is a screenwriter and film producer of both Chinese and English-language films. Chan is a co-founder of the Hong Kong environmental group Green Power and has been a board member of Greenpeace International. He is a co-founder of an active NGO, Minjian International, which connects Chinese intellectuals with their counterparts in other parts of Asia and Africa. His first novel to be translated into English, *The Fat Years*, was published in sixteen countries. He lives in Beijing.

Nicky Harman is a full-time translator of Chinese fiction. She has translated works by Chen Xiwo, Han Dong, Hong Ying, Xinran, Yan Geling, Zhang Ling and Dorothy Tse. She lives in Dorset.

The Fat Years
Chan Koonchung

BEIJING, SOMETIME IN the near future: a month has gone missing from official records. No one has any memory of it, and no one can care less. Except for a small circle of friends, who will stop at nothing to get to the bottom of the sinister cheerfulness and amnesia that has possessed the Chinese nation. When they kidnap a high-ranking official and force him to reveal all, what they learn – not only about their leaders, but also about their own people – stuns them to the core. It is a message that will rock the world . . .

'An all-encompassing metaphor for today's looming superpower . . . a triumph!'
OBSERVER

'Brace, smart and entertaining'
INDEPENDENT

'A not-so-veiled satire of the Chinese government's tendency to make dates such as the Tiananmen massacre virtually disappear'
FINANCIAL TIMES

'This creepy novel frightened me several times . . . because, apart from the missing month, it is mostly true today'
SPECTATOR